Wider Pools

Zee and I were alone in the swimming pool that evening, apart from the black-haired boy. It was a hot summer, the heat went on and on, like the summers of childhood. You think back, your chief memory is the heat. As girls Zee and I used to swim often. She didn't come often now.

It was a small pool, not large enough for diving boards, but quite deep at one end. It was not a well kept place. The wall tiles were cracking, the wood partitions of the changing cubicles were splitting. Insects dropped from the dome. The dry rot gave off a smell. Because of the dry rot the building would have to be pulled down. Next summer the old pool would be gone. I liked it. I felt comfortable there.

BY THE SAME AUTHOR

Endless Race
String Horses
Turnstiles
The Cloud Catchers
Penny Links
Sing About It

Wider Pools

Ursula Holden

Methuen

A Methuen Paperback

WIDER POOLS

ISBN 0 413 53700 5

First published in Great Britain 1983
by Methuen London Ltd

This edition published 1983
by Methuen London Ltd
11 New Fetter Lane, London EC4P 4EE

Made and printed in Great Britain
by The Pitman Press, Bath

One

'Everyone out in ten minutes.'

Zee and I were alone in the swimming pool that evening, apart from the black-haired boy. It was a hot summer, the heat went on and on, like the summers of childhood. You think back, your chief memory is the heat. As girls Zee and I used to swim often. She didn't come often now.

It was a small pool, not large enough for diving boards, but quite deep at one end. It was not a well kept place. The wall tiles were cracking, the wood partitions of the changing cubicles were splitting. Insects dropped from the dome. The dry rot gave off a smell. Because of the dry rot the building would have to be pulled down. Next summer the old pool would be gone. I liked it. I felt comfortable there.

That evening the chlorine was so strong that it made me feel ill and I worried about my eyes. They easily become inflamed. With my hair floating about I felt like a red-eyed mermaid. There was a modern pool at the other end of the bridge, with hygenic changing rooms, showers, a snack-bar. It was close to where Zee lived. I was selfish, she said, to insist on the older pool, but I never forced her to come with me, I was quite happy on my own. I liked the swimmers who came to the old pool, but Zee held blacks in contempt. I liked the shabby streets round about, especially at night. Heat suits black people, they don't get red and cross. The green of the trees shading the streets, the red buses, the vivid cotton clothes seemed more pronounced. It was the summer of ankle-length skirts. The black girls wore beads in their hair. The blossom from the lime trees fell thickly on the pavements, sweetening the smell of petrol and sweat. There were fears of water shortage, ruined crops, death from heatstroke.

I floated on my back, waiting for Zee to leave her cubicle. Another beetle fell from the glass dome into a lock of my hair. At last Zee stepped awkwardly down.

'We've only just got here. Why does he want to close?'

'You take so long to undress.' I was always in first; I wore my costume under my dress, to save time changing.

She swam heavily, flailing her large arms. Her face in her petalled bathing-cap looked lumpy and irritable.

'Everyone out in five minutes.' The attendant looked at Zee, his expression was mocking. The black-haired boy at the other end watched her too. He climbed up the metal steps, jumping in with a huge splash, showering Zee's face and cap. She was nearly eight years older than I. Approaching middle age now, she was fat. We both loved food. I was lucky, I had always been thin. At school she had been ashamed of having such a skinny sister. She was envious now. She looked like a whale when she swam. She shook her face free of water, scowling at the boy. Then she scowled at me, as if I were to blame. I hoped she wouldn't want to walk home with me, I liked walking home alone, especially after a swim. Swimming was calming and I liked the empty streets. Zee had a husband, Ted. She envied me my freedom though she depended on Ted. I resented her bossiness. At school we'd been scholarship girls. We used to envy the girls from wealthy backgrounds. She had lost no time in marrying Ted when she left. Ted kept her in comfort. She despised me for not marrying. She envied me my looks. Heat didn't suit her. I never reddened or tanned, I looked after my skin. I have always loved the sun. Zee had kept the affected accent she had picked up at school.

'What an impertinent man. He keeps staring. He's so *rude*.'

'He's only a holiday relief. I don't let him bother me.'

I didn't like his face either, a mean-eyed, mean-mouthed face, with hair the colour of ash. His teeth were sharp and wet.

The black-haired boy jumped again, splashing

Zee over the face again.

'You don't own the pool. Keep away from me.'

The boy smiled nervously, showing small, prominent teeth. She shouted again. A beetle plopped near her mouth. I put my feet down. I could just stand on tip-toe.

'You shouldn't be angry, Zee. That boy goes to my school. I'm not sure of his name.'

'Immigrant rubbish. I can't think why you stay there.'

'They aren't all immigrants, Zee. There are some white children.'

'Most of them are black. You know my feelings.'

'Everyone out now. That means you, ma'am. If you can manage it.' The attendant's voice was sibilant, a whispering watery voice that carried. He was talking to Zee. The black-haired boy got out, going to his cubicle the other side of the pool.

'Insolence. I'd like to report him. I wish you'd stop coming here, Shirley.'

I went on floating for a last moment. She was right, he had spoiled our swim. The usual supervisor often gave us extra swimming time. He blew a whistle, he never shouted. I felt dreamy. The water bubbled in my hair. The black-haired boy left his cubicle, young and serious again, wearing dark jeans and tee shirt.

'Come on, you. I said out. You in the deep end. Move it.'

Zee climbed out haughtily, the water sucked at

her costume, making it wrinkle like skin. At the top of the metal steps she paused, whale-like, the water running down her in streams. She had been humiliated, she banged her cubicle door. I went into mine, next to hers. I hooked the green canvas flap across the top of the door. The flap was for extra privacy, to stop people looking in. The design of the pool, the air of decay, the beetles that fell on your head gave it character. The smell of chlorine from the water was so strong that day that it drowned the smell of feet and old knickers inside my cubicle. My eyes hurt. On the bench someone had left a crumpled corn plaster with blood on it. I dressed myself standing up, not liking to sit on the bench. I fished my sandal from the gulley where it had fallen. The chlorine smell clung to my hair, my clothes, my hands. I heard the attendant opening and shutting the cubicle doors, checking each one for lost property. Usually there were three men on duty, tonight it was just him and the cashier. The tiles round the pool had to be hosed, because of the beetles. I heard him dragging the hose.

Zee whispered, 'Secure your canvas flap. He'll probably try to look in.'

'Why should he? He's in charge.'

'I don't trust him, or that boy. They're probably in league.'

I told her she was fussing as I shook out my hair, but I felt uneasy. As he passed he kicked the bloodied corn plaster from the gulley back under my door. Soon the dome would be dark. The water was already a darker blue, too dark to see the beetles. I left my cubicle, treading on something that crunched. The tiles were slippery with wet. The swing doors leading from the pool were open and I could hear the cashier counting her money in her booth. She hummed as she stacked the piles of coins under the light of an unshaded bulb. The sight of her was reassuring.

'Where are the rest of the staff tonight, the usual ones?'

'Boss left early. Temporary man say go home to the others.'

'It's early to close now. I wonder why he's doing that?'

'Don't know, miss. Temporary man say close.'

He was clicking the pool lights off as Zee joined me. She said it was against the law to run the pool short of staff, it was risking accidents. I couldn't help wishing she didn't look so fat and hot. In spite of her petalled cap her hair had got wet. It stuck out now round her face rather like sticky quills. Bits of the shiny black cap poked through the mesh of her string bag.

'I watched that man as you walked round the pool. He couldn't take his eyes off you. How *do* you manage it, Shirley?'

'Manage what?' Her jealousy and sarcasm made me nervous. I would rather be jealous of someone than have them be jealous of me. Zee had a comfortable home and Ted, she had never been poor or had bad health, but she wasn't a happy woman.

'I'd be ashamed to be ogled the way he ogled

you. What's the secret, Shirley?'

'There is no secret. I didn't notice him. Besides, you have Ted, he adores you.'

'Oh him.'

She held so many people in contempt. Poor people, black people, Ted. She was always complaining of me yet she seemed to need me as much as she needed Ted. I don't think she loved me. I would have been fonder of her if she didn't criticize. At home we had been poor, it was the school that changed Zee. Our father had been a bus conductor. She never referred to him. She left home when she left school and never went back again. For years I lost all contact with her until recently when she'd moved to London. We fell into the habit of meeting at the pool, though she complained of the district, saying it was a slum. We had a need for each other that was more than our shared blood. I suppose both us were lonely in different ways.

The steps outside the pool were used as a meeting point for the local youths. They stared at passers by, shouted and joked together. A few wore baggy caps to cover their springy hair. On the bottom step was a pile of jackets, patterned with metal studs. The black-haired boy stood near, watching. He was much younger, not as dark, his hair was sleek and straight. When he saw me he smiled, his teeth white in the twilight. I'd often seen him at school, had noticed how quiet and shy he was, always watching, never in a group. He took his swimming seriously, always alone, swimming up and down the pool, breathing heavily. I admire persistence. I felt sorry for him. Outside in the street it felt hotter still. Zee sniffed as she walked down the steps. Black trash, scum, not worth bothering about.

'I like them. Somebody has to care. They're people, like you and me.'

I had worked at the local school for years, first as a kitchen help, now as assistant cook, a job which Zee held in contempt. I got satisfaction from seeing the children's faces when they ate what I'd helped to make. My baked brown sugar roll with orange custard was a favourite. I think that Zee, who had no children, was jealous of my contact with them, though she said she never regretted being childless. Had she had a family she might have been less cantankerous. She might even have been less fat. She rarely mentioned Ted. We both had left the school without sitting any exams. I thought of her as someone with an undeveloped soul.

We walked down the street. The black youths watched us. I knew she wanted to come home with me. I liked being on my own, I was used to it. That summer I wanted to swim alone, walk alone, keep to myself until the term started again. I walked slightly ahead, hearing her panting behind.

'Shall we buy an ice?' she called.

'In the long run they make you feel hotter.'

'I'll get a cone. Go on.'

She loved sweet things, she wanted the excuse. She ate three choc ices while I licked the cone. Then she drank tins of cola, having peeled back the ring tops and stowed them in her string bag. She'd always been tidy. Our mother used to predict that I'd never make a wife, I was too slapdash. Zee was different. Long ago we used to imagine winning a prince charming who would place us in a palace filled with children. I think we hoped to share the prince, the palace as well as the children. Now, as a cook in a school which catered mostly for West Indian children, I think I was happier than her. She wiped her fingers on a corner of her towel, having primly wiped her mouth. She would have another ice if I would.

'I must get back. You eat one, though.'

She ate quickly, her tongue flicking round her mouth. I found her greediness rather endearing, it reduced her superiority. She made little to effort to curb it, food gave her such pleasure. I smiled when we reached the traffic lights, the parting of our ways.

'Don't go yet, Shirley. I don't feel very well.'

I stepped aside just in time as she vomited on to the pavement. The look in her eyes was more shamed than surprised. She heaved a second time. Instead of feeling sorry for her, I was cross.

'Oh stop, Zee. You shouldn't be sick in public.'

She shook her head and bent over. When she stood up her face was the same shade as the pool oozing into the gutter. She swayed. I didn't want to pity her. My sickly whale of a sister was an embarrassment. I put up my hand for a taxi. The driver looked down in distaste. I pulled his door open and pushed Zee inside. I avoided her shamed-looking eyes. I was abandoning her. I couldn't stand the sight of her, the good of my swim was undone. I didn't wait for the taxi to turn, I'd done all I was going to do. As I ran towards my street I thought I saw the boy with the black hair standing on the corner. I ran up my staircase. As I was putting my key into my door my telephone started ringing. I guessed that it would be Zee.

'A fine sister you are. Fancy leaving me. Fancy letting me *go*'.

'If I'd been sick in the street, I would rather be left alone.'

'You could have come with me. You could have telephoned.'

'I haven't had a chance. I've just got home.'

'I've been so sick. You're cold-hearted.'

'You ought to got to bed.'

As children, she'd been the one to nurse me, to protect me. I was letting her down.

'I wish you were here, Shirley.'

'Ted is home, isn't he?'

'*Him*.'

'I'll ring you tomorrow to find out how you are.'

'What are you hiding, Shirley? You're so secretive.'

'I can't help it. I'm always quiet. I like to be alone.'

'You behave as if you were on another plane. Why won't you come to France with us on Friday? I wish you would change your mind.'

'We've been into that. I want to be here. You won't need me once you are there.'

'Please.'

'It's too late. I've already made other plans.'

Every August they went to the same hotel in Calais. A month of sun in the company of middle-aged English visitors was their idea of bliss. I longed for her to be gone.

'Ted wants you to come. I'm sorry I snapped at you.'

I told her to take care of herself. I wouldn't change my mind. While she and Ted were away I was going to start writing a book. I'd been collecting notes and old diaries for years. This summer I would get to work.

Two

I have always had an interest in cooking. I didn't have a free rein at work. At home I experimented. I like to invent my own recipes. That evening I decided to make pasta with an unusual sauce, something with a strong taste to combat the chlorine. I would forget Zee's vomiting and think about myself. My eyelids still stung. I leaned out of the window in my bathroom, hoping for a breeze. The window opened on to a fire escape. Below me the back lane was quiet. In the day time you could hear hammering and shouts from the repair shops. Old bicycles and washing machines changed hands in the back lane. You often heard paint sprays hiss. It was a haunt for rogues. If you leaned far enough you could see the dome of the old swimming pool catching the sunlight. Tonight there was nothing to see except low clouds shifting and merging. Later there would be a new moon.

I went to the kitchen to start the sauce. I ran the tap while I peeled the onions. They say running water lessens the fumes. They were old onions, sprouting with green, the outer skins had gone soft. I chopped the good parts, mixing them with spice. In spite of the running water, my eyes, reddened from chlorine, started running again. I may be untidy and slapdash but I love my home. My furniture is all second hand, some of it I bought in the back lane. I love my divan and old sofa which I have covered in butcher blue hessian. Dark blue, white and all shades of red are my favourites. I like coloured ceilings. I sliced an apple into the onion mixture and some shredded coconut. Coconut gives interest to any savoury mix. When the mixture was in the pan I added the grated cheese and an egg yolk, turning the gas low. I put a lot of spaghetti into boiling water; I like a big meal at night. I was washing my hands when I heard an odd puffing sound. I'm uneasy when I hear sighs and groans because, being a poor sleeper, I have unpleasant dreams. My worst dream is the one where I'm being chased, something is trying to drown me and I always wake myself up with my own breathing. I turned off the tap, the sound came from the hall. My pan was bubbling, the cheese smell was filling the air. My kitchen and bathroom are on either side of the front door which is opposite my bedsitting room overlooking the main road. I stood in the hall. The flap of my letterbox was lifting and falling, though there was no wind. I stopped. I held up the flap. Something rubbery and pink was outside making a noise at me. I put my eye close to the gap. Two holes like two nostrils in a snout were snorting the other side. There was a choke and then silence. I opened the door and a kneeling figure almost toppled in. It was the boy with black hair, wearing a rubber mask that fitted him as tightly as skin. Heavy rubber brows shaded the eye holes. I could see his eyes shining. He had great rubber ears.

'Take off that nonsense and stand up. I know who you are. What the hell are you playing at?'

He pulled off the mask. He looked at the floor.

'Why are you here?'

'I seen you at the school, miss. Cooking.'

He seemed frightened. His lashes were so curly they almost touched his lids. He was tall but he didn't seem to be more than about six. His hands and feet were small though he had long limbs. He tangled his hands together unhappily.

'So? What do you want?'

'Just looking, miss. Just wanting to find out . . .'

'Find out what?'

'Find where you lived.'

'How old are you?''

'Seven . . . nearly seven.'

It had just been a silly prank, not naughtiness. He looked so afraid.

'Were you trying to scare me?'

'I just wanted to see in. I saw your friend, the other lady, saw her getting sick. Is she bad?'

'Why were you wearing a mask? What were you trying to do?'

'I . . . didn't want you to see me. I wasn't . . . naughty.' He tried to grin, his poking teeth were touching. He didn't have the sing-song accent of most West Indians, nor was he very dark skinned.

'What's your name? It isn't very funny trying to frighten people with monkey masks. It isn't kind.'

'Manuel. I seen you at the pool. I like swimming.'

'I know. I've watched you. What else do you like doing?'

'Buses. I'd like to drive a bus.'

'My father was with the buses.'

'What does "genesis" mean, miss?'

' "Genesis"? That's a strange word for you to use. It's a beginning. The start of something. Why, where did you hear it?'

He said he thought it was on the radio. He licked his lip nervously, twisting his fingers again. I felt sorry for him. I wanted to be kind to him, not bully him. He was always hanging round older children or swimming by himself. The pan of spaghetti spat on to the stove.

'Whatever you wanted here, I'm feeling hungry. My supper is ready. Would you like something to eat?'

I had never had a child from the school inside my home, or any child at all. He looked frail and excited standing inside my hall. Steam came from the kitchen. He looked round at the white walls, the orange ceiling and blue carpeting. He whispered that it looked pretty.

'I'm glad you like it. I love orange and blue. I've been making a new kind of sauce. Do you like pasta?'

He was confused. He had frightened me, now I was frightening him. A child alone is vulnerable. I showed him where he could wash. I heard him run the taps in the bathroom, the sounds of water gurgling, the toilet being flushed. When he came out he still had the towel in his hand. He had washed his face, his lashes sparkled, wet drops were in his hair. The nape of his neck was damp and I felt warm towards him, glad I had asked him in. He sat on a stool and looked down at his plate.

'Do you like using a knife and fork? Are you used to spaghetti?'

'I never tried. What is it?'

I showed him how to wind lengths of spaghetti round his fork, but he preferred his knife, cutting his food into short lengths, eating it tidily. He was a proud boy in spite of shyness. He said he liked the food, but he was more used to chips. The kitchen was filled with the cooking smell mixed with the soap he'd been using, orange scented.

'Would you like an apple?'

I showed him how to cut the peel off in a single length before throwing it on to the floor. It was supposed to shape into the initial of the one you would one day love.

'"S". Looks like an "S", miss. Your turn now. You throw.'

I said that I was too old for such things now, I

had other concerns. Too old? The undying love from the prince, the castle, the children that Zee and I used to dream about had lost its magic. I thought of my mother crying, my father's indifference, the rows. The strongest memory of love had been in the dreams we had made.

'Try. Please. Go on, miss.'

My peel formed a rough question-mark.

I didn't ask Manuel about his home, I would wait until he volunteered. Having finished eating he was less diffident, his face looked less forlorn. He took an orange, cutting the peel into the shape of teeth, changing his mouth into a monstrous orange grin. Through distorted lips he said that he wouldn't mind teaching swimming. And he liked watching birds as well.

'My neighbour, Mr Caige, who lives on the other side of the landing, has a parrot. Perhaps you'll see it one day.'

'Parrots live a long time. They talk if you teach them. Does your friend, that other lady, does she live here?'

'She isn't a friend, she's my sister. She lives with her husband. On Friday she's going to France. Is that why you came, to ask me how she was?'

He blinked, looking trapped again. He tore the orange peel teeth into pieces. I showed him how to squeeze the pieces so that the oil ran, a lovely orange smell on your hands. I wondered if his mother was worried about him. I'd been wrong, I supposed, to ask him in. As if he read my thoughts he said he'd better be leaving now. He'd like to see that parrot. Could he use the orange soap again? He liked the shape of it. He didn't say goodbye before he left, but looked over his shoulder, a look of longing and regret. I cleared the table. I shouldn't have mentioned the parrot. I had to have time to myself, without ties. He might demand more of me than I was prepared to give.

I brushed my hair in front of the bathroom window. My hair was my best feature, also my eyes. My pointy face stared back from the mirror. I had strong short lashes, the whites of my eyes were clear. When I bathed them in eye lotion, opening them into the blue eyebath, it was like a crystal ball. The past beckoned. ('Dream-eyes, those eyes were made to love', 'Love me a little, I look in your eyes and drown', 'forget-me-not eyes, remember?') Too old? Could I, would I love? When I looked in the mirror again my eyes were the same blue as the eyebath.

I like music when I go to sleep, especially when I'm tired. A tenor voice on the radio sang the same song as the cashier had sung earlier. 'If I were a blackbird I'd whistle and sing, I'd follow the ship that my true love sailed in.' I lay on my divan, I couldn't get the boy's face out of my mind. I hoped I would sleep without dreaming. When I looked through half-closed eyes at the patch of light at the end of my divan, the shape looked like a man. I like to imagine shapes, I see faces in rug weaving, animals in cracks in the wall, monsters in soap bubbles. I slept without realizing, though it cannot have been for long; the same song was still going on. I knew before opening my eyes that I wasn't alone. A man was standing where the shape of light had been. A real man, not an imaginary one; standing there, watching me. First the boy with the black hair, Manuel, now this man creeping up the fire escape like a monkey. When I spoke it was a whisper.

'What are you doing? Please leave.'

I put on the bedside light. It was the man from the swimming pool with the wet teeth and ash-coloured hair. He wore a cord jacket now, with matching, snuff-coloured slacks. His shirt, opened to the waist, showed a bony, sunken-in chest. He looked amused.

'Beg pardoney for the intrusion. I knocked and I rang. I heard your music, knew you must be in.'

'What do you want please?'

'I came to say something. The boy said you lived here. He lives . . . near my block of flats. I don't know your number or I would have phoned. I went round to the back, I saw you brushing your hair.'

'You spied on me. You climbed up the fire escape.'

'I wanted to talk to you, miss. Beg pardoney a lot. I'm often round the back. I got good friends there.'

'Talk about what? I've nothing to say to you.'

'It's about the plant. The plant at the swimming pool. One of the cylinders, one of the MSVs was leaking. Not dangerous at all, not serious.'

'You mean the chlorine regulator? I thought something was wrong. What happened to the others? Where were the rest of the staff?'

'Boss went home. I did the best I could, I said they could all leave before I found what was wrong.'

'My sister was quite ill. You ought to be fired for this.'

'I'm just a temp man, you know, leaving end of the week. The maintenance men can fix it. Everything will be alrighty.'

'You could have caused serious harm.'

'That's why I come here now. To say it's harmless, just a small inconvenience.'

'Inconvenience? First the boy comes sniffing through my letterbox. Now you come breaking in. You should be fired. I thought something was wrong, my eyes hurt so.'

'I'm only a temp man, you know. I'm leaving end of the week. Sorry, miss, ever so.'

'It's disgraceful.'

'I'm sorry about your eyes. Blue eyes, lovely eyes. You ain't bashful though, not as bashful as you make out. Oh no. Got a temper too.'

He put his hand out. I pulled mine away. His hand felt scaly.

'Bastard.'

His face changed, he went quiet. Then he shrugged. He said to be careful who I called that name. He knew all about me. Oh yes.

'Get out of here.'

'Sorry I disturbed your beauty sleep. Don't get lonely, will you.'

He showed his wet teeth in a leer and left.

I got up and bolted the door after him. I bolted the bathroom window. Now I knew why Zee had been ill. It hadn't been the ice creams, it was the chlorine. He'd closed early because he'd been afraid. Zee might have died. Poor Zee, I'd deserted her.

When I lay down again it was my turn to feel ill. I tried to fight the giddiness and nausea. The nasturtium-coloured ceiling started to spin about and I was as sick as she had been earlier.

Three

I forgot everything but the misery of sickness. My forehead and palms were wet, my eyes started running again. I sat groaning on the edge of the bath. Light rain was falling outside, sounding like fingers touching the window pane. Earlier I had been annoyed with Zee, now I was annoyed with myself. I hadn't got time to be ill, I had too much on my mind. I ran a bath. I thought about Manuel again as I rolled the cake of orange soap in my hands. I would have a hot soak and forget about stomach poisoning. I rubbed the soap behind my ears, under my arms, I smoothed the skin between my little toes, pampering myself with oils, soft creams, massage. I poured jugfuls of hot water over my head. I attended every inch. Later I would drink herbal tea and forget about the old swimming pool and the man with the ash-coloured hair. I wouldn't tell Zee about my visitors. She was excitable, she'd only make a fuss. She would want to come round, cancel her holiday even. It was just possible that the sickness had been a summer germ or the ice cream we'd had in the street.

I decided to change my room round. My divan would go in the window, my butcher blue sofa behind the door. I would face the table to the wall, to avoid distraction while I started work on my book. It would be a novel, based on my life but with a difference. I would change what I hadn't liked. I would keep Zee in it, but there'd be no mention of our home or our real parents. The father who had shamed his daughters by visiting the grammar school in his busman's uniform would become an architect. The mother who had dropped her aitches, weeping in front of the head, would be an opera singer. There'd be no parental split with Zee escaping to marry Ted. No mention of lost loves or the jobs I'd done. I wanted to forget about being a hostess, a cleaner, or working in a hospital canteen. The book I'd write would be the kind of life I would have chosen, the kind I deserved. A short work in first-person prose about two middle-class sisters who lead a charmed life. I'd omit what had caused me pain. I'd keep my looks, my likes and dislikes. I'd certainly change Zee's appearance. By inventing and fabricating a past my future would improve. I'd think more of myself. I didn't want to publish it, just change the way I felt. Pretended happenings can feel real if you invent hard enough. By the end of the book I'd be changed. I had told no one about it, particularly Zee. If she knew she might want to be my secretary. I pushed my furniture round, the place of work was important. I would buy something new to wear, get my hair cut. Uncut since I was fourteen, it now grew to my waist. The tips were golden, darkening a little at the roots. I had no style in mind, just something different. I hadn't been in a hairdresser for almost fifteen years.

'Short, please. An easy, casual style.'

The salon was for older women, intent on recapturing their past. I was fortunate, I had a future, my past was being cut out. The women waited their turn to be primped and tweezed, their curls rinsed through with dye. I was different.

'You sure, dear? Seems a shame when you've had it so long. I could do it up in curls. Dyed is it? *Really*? You don't often see that shade. Reminds me of my goldfish. I have two, Darby and Joan.'

'Quite sure.' And I'll have you know, you elderly beautician with bleached hair and brows, that I'm natural, not like you. I'm beautiful, I'm real, I'm not corseted out of shape. You don't realize what you're doing. You're snipping my old life away. I can't watch it, can't open my eyes. When those money-greedy scissors stop snipping I'll have a new future, new self. I want my hair short. I do not want to look.

'Something in your eye, dear? Need a towel? Most probably a titchy bit of hair.'

'Thank you. I'll do it, give me the towel, please.'

Stop watching me, Madam Bleach. Your concern is as unreal as the flowers on your smock, as false as your unloving heart. My hair, my lovely hair. Men have desired it, touched it, kissed it. Have you been desired, Madam Bleach, you with the cruel stare? Your eyes belie you, you haven't been desired.

'All right, dear? No regrets, I hope? Not upset about it? I've left a bit of fullness in front, here, where you need it. The front gets thinner first. Got kiddies, dear? No? Thought not, you can usually tell.'

You're saying I'm bald, I'm ageing, that I'm barren and undesired, you with the greedy scissors, hard eyes and elderly goldfish in a bowl.

'There now, dear, how's that? Take a look, open your eyes. I'll hold the mirror for you, can you see the back?'

I'm a girl again, I'm young. I have a fringe again. I am beginning now.

'Some studs in your ears, pearl ones would suit you. Make you a bit up to date. Like mine, dear. And . . . dear . . . what about your eyes? "Purple Bruise" shadow is what I wear. My lipstick is "Passionate Plum".'

'No thanks. I never wear make-up, I never have, I'm not starting now.'

You metal woman, you mean well. Your scissors have worked well. I'm ready, I'm starting now.

She moved to another client, lifting the drier from a dyed, well heated head. A little more fullness in front, the front does get thinner first. Got grand-kiddies have you? Thought not, I can usually tell. I watched her lift the darkened wisps of hair round her comb, her metal eyes calculating, suggesting.

A bus conductor shouted. 'Hey, buttercup, come for a ride.'

Another man bumped me purposely. The magic worked. Next I would buy a dress, and boots with satin tops. Red boots with heels and legs high over the knees and perhaps a chiffon scarf, or a smock with ethnic sleeves that slipped up my forearms. I'd buy earrings with glittery stones, long ones, and orange scent.

'You half fare, miss, or are you Puss in Boots?'

The best cosmetic, the loveliest garment of all is flattery. I don't feel like a school cook now. What matters most is how you feel inside. I ought to be kinder to Zee, I have so much. I feel free.

I decided to go to Victoria, to wave her off to France, give their trip my blessing, though not my company. Zee needed me still, she always had. When she was young she'd found being alone intolerable, she'd minded our parents rows more than I had. We never spoke about them, preferring our fantasy world. When she left to marry Ted I had no one until I left school myself and got away. I used to listen to my shouting parents at night. Worse than the shouting had been their heaving breathing and pants in the night. I slept in the room next door. I couldn't understand my mother, crying during the day because of my father's moods, yet at night her pantings were evidently from delight. I never told Zee about it. She'd never shown any curiousity about my life after she left home. Ted was her ticket of escape. Now back in London she simply thought I should stop being a cook and work at something with more prestige. I didn't feel in the least lowly inside or outside now. I wanted to show Zee my boots. I decided not to tell her, I'd make it a surprise.

I left my flat early on Friday, wearing my new, tiered skirt. The air felt damp and cool on my newly-bared neck. My red-stone earrings clicked. She was by the bookstall looking at magazines. She liked articles on housecraft, plain recipes for plain dishes, economical tips for the home. I glanced over her shoulder. 'Flooding. What and what not to do.' She didn't see me.

Ted was with the luggage, waiting for Zee. He seemed tired. His Adam's apple resting on his collar was as thinly yellow as the skin around his eyes. His *Times* was under the same arm that held his stick.

'Sister Shirley, you look wonderful. What a surprise. You've changed your mind, you're joining us?'

'I just came to see you off.'

'You're different. What have you done?'

'My hair. Do you like it?'

'It . . . you look about sixteen years old.'

'I'm changing. This is my summer of change. Is the boat train in?'

'Platform twelve. You could still come. Do, Shirley, it would please Zee so much. I'll pay for you gladly. Say yes.'

I thanked him. It was out of the question. I felt sorry for him, he would do anything for Zee who treated him with contempt. She ran her home like clockwork, she didn't know how to cherish anyone. When he called her she jumped. Her face lit when she saw me, before freezing into disbelief. She blinked exaggeratedly at my hair.

'To what do we owe the honour? Has the Lady Shirley changed her mind? And what have we done to our *hair*? I don't like it, I can't say it suits you at all.'

'Ted likes it, don't you, Ted? I'm pleased with it myself.'

She didn't mention my clothes, her eyes showed what she felt about them. Ted said he'd been trying to persuade me to change my mind. It seemed that I had other plans.

'Oh I believe you, Ted. Plans she's too secretive to tell us about. Too busy to telephone her own sister when she was ill. Too busy trying to make herself young. I don't care for the earrings.'

'Zee, I've been ill too, you know.'

I was sick of her possessiveness, sick of her malice, her need. She hadn't grown up inside. She looked uglier. Her suit was too tight, her hair was awful. She should never wear that shade of green or such pointed shoes. I couldn't help being better-looking. I couldn't help being thin. I wanted her to love me and be proud of me, I wanted to be proud of her. She sniffed. She didn't believe I'd been ill.

'I only came to say goodbye to you both. I thought you would be pleased.'

'Goodbye then. Come along, Ted.'

She looked triumphant, she had spoiled my plan and had the final word. She could leave on the arm of her husband who kept her in comfort. But at the barrier she looked back, her face uncertain again. She would miss me. I had wanted to tell her not to eat any ice cream or drink any tap water in France.

That night I had a telephone call. A voice whispered and breathed heavily.

'Oh Shirley. Shir—ley. Who's been a naughty girl, then? I know what you did.'

I guessed it was the man from the pool with the wet teeth and ash-coloured hair. He didn't frighten me. How did he know? Had I been naughty? I had done what seemed best at the time.

Four

I suppose the telephone call that night made me dream about Tina. She had managed the club where I worked years ago, in Ladbroke Grove. She had looked after me, had shown me what to do. I went there when I left school and our parents had parted. There were three hostesses; Tina, Pauline and me. The club owner, Al, was Tina's boyfriend who was often away. He didn't care what went on as long as the club made money. It wasn't plushy, just a bar, a few tables and a tiny square floor to dance on to recorded music. Tina, Pauline and I got a percentage of the takings. The barmen, relatives of Al's usually, never stayed at the club for long. Our job was to welcome the clients, dance with them, above all to get them to drink. After closing we could do as we liked, keep anything we earned. It was Tina who taught me how to flatter men, how to get them to spend. I didn't drink much, nor did Pauline. We used to pretend that our glasses contained whisky instead of ginger ale. Tina liked gin. My love of cooking now may have stemmed from the club days, where no food was served, just drink. Pauline and I were always hungry. We had to dress well, not get drunk and keep the clients spending. It was Tina they came to see, her red hair, blue sequins and paint were eye-catching. Pauline was an upper-class girl who wore classic dresses. She had a beautiful speaking voice. I liked artistic clothes, velvet slacks, interesting shoes and never any make-up. The three of us got on well, we had to, we were thrown together so much. We used to swap experiences and give each other advice. Pauline had had a baby and a sad life, dogged by bad luck. The father of her child had burned to death in their flat, her baby died later. Her own father had been a colonel, she'd been taught by a governess and loved dancing. Tina's background was similar to my own except that she'd seen little of her Dad. The life in Ladbroke Grove was seedy and I took to it easily. Anything was better than home. I didn't tell my family, like Zee I disappeared. From Tina I learned flattery. From Pauline I learned to listen. Once clients could trust you, they started doubling their drinks. Pauline was sincere, she preferred truth, that's why she didn't speak much. Pauline and I worried about Tina's drinking. She said that gin stopped you getting pregnant. Al was away when I got pregnant, he knew nothing about it. Tina was angry with me. I should have told her before it was too late to stop it. She didn't want me to leave. She said babies ruined your life, look at Pauline, she'd had one, had tried to keep it, when it died she'd gone nervy and strange, she hardly ever spoke. Tina said I shouldn't think of keeping it, do what she said, she'd help me out. No need for nurses and doctors, she'd see to the whole thing herself. Upstairs in the flat where we lived, she'd help me, find a home for the child. She knew about births all right, had helped her mother often enough. I trusted her, I obeyed her. In the room in the flat upstairs she took charge. She told me to breathe in, trust her, to breathe what she held to my face. The smell of it, the vile stench, the nausea was what I remembered most. The smell of what Tina held to my face was worse than the pain of the birth. I never saw the child, I just remember the smell. She shouted at me. 'Breathe will you, breathe in, you silly cow.' Then nothing, blankness. I woke in a bed of blood. The room was empty. When Tina came back she had blood on her skirt, blood in her fingernails. She got angry when I questioned, she wouldn't answer me. I wanted Pauline, but she'd left by that time. I begged, I screamed, I threatened. Don't ask any questions, just a baby. Forget it now, you asked me to help you, I did. Boy or girl? Don't ask me, forget it. It's gone. Twins? Dead? Deformed? Stop, Shirl. it's over and done. You didn't want it, I said I'd help, I'm your friend.

I left after a few days, left Ladbroke Grove for

good. I didn't say goodbye. I even left most of my clothes behind, the velvet slacks, the interesting beaded shoes, the necklaces, in the dingy flat upstairs. I moved from the district. I never let myself think of that time, I made a new life for myself. I did cleaning, I worked in a hospital canteen, I made myself forget. Then I joined the school where I worked now. 'Who's been a naughty girl, then?' Not naughty. I did what seemed best at the time.

And Tina came into my dream. You can't control dreams, she was there. Her vivid hair, her staring turquoise eyes were there, red-mouthed in the swimming pool. Then Manuel swam by with his mask, splashing us, crying from the eyeholes, wet running down his rubber cheeks. The whispering voice called out, 'Everyone out in five minutes'. I heard that breathing again. I woke then, I was crying. That life was gone, past, finished. There was before Ladbroke Grove and afterwards. I was different. I had changed and was still changing. I was a flat occupier in my own right, school cook with aspirations. I had Zee as a friend again, though we saw life differently and we argued. I wanted to finish my book. I got up, I went to my typewriter. I'd put in a new ribbon in readiness. Write something. Listen to your heart. My heart died a long time ago, in that room in Ladbroke Grove. Zee's heart never developed, my own died before it learned love. Onions, basil, coconut, a spoonful of Earl Grey tea. I have only my present and future, to think of my past is pain.

I'll think about Zee and Ted, in France now, asleep in twin beds. Twin beds, separated by a reading lamp, a travelling clock, Ted's folded *Times*. Dressing-gown above neatly-placed slippers. Silence, boredom, peace.

I slept poorly. In the morning a telegram arrived. 'TED VERY ILL. WILL TELEPHONE MIDDAY.' I was furious. Zee's undeveloped soul was reaching to me from France, she wouldn't be shut away. Selfish, clinging, needful Zee. I didn't have to answer the telephone. I did answer it.

'Is that you, Shirley? It's Ted, he's had a stroke. You must help me, Shirley. Are you there? Can you hear?'

'I'm here, I'm busy, Zee. I can't come. Has Ted seen a doctor?'

'I don't trust these French doctors, jabbering and waving their hands. They're no help. I want you.'

'Are you certain it is a stroke? How bad is he? I mean, truthfully.'

'He's bad. I'm really worried.'

I kept repeating that I couldn't come. She broke down, the line crackled with lamentation. I reasoned, I tried to be firm. Ted needed *her*, not me. I knew that I would go, Zee would win. I wanted to free myself, yet I wanted to be pulled back. Her sobbing enraged me. Also it upset me.

'Stop crying, it won't help.'

'I . . . can't . . . I'm . . . so worried.'

I stopped arguing. I told her I'd join them for one day. I'd take a day trip, they could return with me or not, depending on how Ted was. Her sobbing stopped. She made a pretence then of considering me. I mustn't come unless I really wanted. She'd hate to put me out.

'I've said I'll come and I will. I'll let you know the time after I've booked.'

She babbled. I was her angel, her good samaritan. She'd *known* I wouldn't let her down. France was all right for a holiday, but no good for illness at all. For illness you needed your own bed in your own country, with your own sister nearby. What time would I come? Make it early. Poor old Ted, he *would* be pleased.

I rang the travel agency. I'd never left England before.

Five

It was still hot but the dry spell had broken. A steady drizzle fell. Victoria Station was packed. It seemed that the whole of London was there, pushing, shouting, worrying. I looked for the boat-train queue, I looked for hands that held visas as well as tickets. Luggage lay everywhere, impeding the ankles and knees. Older travellers looked vainly for porters. In high summer you had to resign yourself, you carried your own bags or else you stayed at home. Red-faced mothers shouted. Children with crisps or lollies in their hands ignored them. It made sense to stock up with nosh before you reached abroad. Frog's legs, snails, red wine were all very well, you could be sure of the station grub. There was a smell of diesel.

I was going to be firm, stick to my decision to return that night. I had brought no night clothes, nothing except some notes for my book. I would go over them as I journeyed. My red boots matched my skirt and my earrings. I smelled of orange perfume. I had seen Zee off so many times, now I was joining the throng. I'd forgotten to tell Mr Caige that I would be back late. He took in my milk and kept an eye on the landing. I had a dread of flooding and fires since Pauline had told me about her burning basement, her burned boyfriend, the soaked ruins after the firemen had left. She would always be haunted by the smell of burned clothing, burned furniture, the smell of singed flesh. I was going to France for the first time, I wouldn't think of anything else. Soon I would be enjoying the countryside of Kent. I would enjoy France, I would stop blaming Zee. I loved my new skirt, brushing the tops of my boots; my hair was exactly right. I pushed through a group of children, giggling and dropping crumbs. I found the end of the queue. A woman in front was shouting.

'This caper is costing me, Manny. Look happy, can't you? Stop messing about.'

I stared. My heart jerked. I had dreamed about Tina. She was standing in front of me. The black-haired boy with his back to me was Manuel. There was no mistaking his hair, his nervous, long-fingered hands. He was wearing a broadcloth suit, big on the shoulders. His feet were laced into scuffed black shoes. I had recognized Tina's voice.

'Tina. It is Tina?'

'Pardon? Who are you?'

Manuel smiled at me. 'Hullo, miss.' He turned towards Tina. 'It's the lady from the school. She does the dinners.'

'Oh yeah? How d'you do.'

'It's so strange. I dreamed about you.'

'Dreamed? What about?'

'You do remember me, don't you? Remember Shirl? Ladbroke Grove?'

'That's right. So you are. That's a while ago now. How've you been going on? Your voice ain't changed.'

Her hair was still brilliantly red, reddened with henna now. She looked much older, still interesting in a battered way. She reminded me of a market person, loud-voiced, with knowing eyes. She hadn't smiled at me, she didn't appear pleased. I wanted to question her at once. If I knew what she'd done with my child, I might lose some of my guilt. Her eyes were cold, she avoided my eyes. Beside Manuel was a small girl, chewing her hair.

'I'm glad you haven't changed, Tina.'

'Before you start asking questions, just you remember, we agreed. No trips down memory lane. Got it?'

'I remember. But Tina . . .'

'No buts. Just because you bump into me accidental doesn't change anything. No questions. You weren't following me by any chance? Why're you here?'

'Of course not. I never expected to see you again. Manuel goes to the school where I work. I've seen him swimming too. I'm glad to see you.'

'Likewise I'm sure. Only I don't want no trouble, see? Shake hands, Manny.'

He looked different in his baggy suit. I decided not to mention his visit to me, wearing a monkey mask. I asked if she lived in London still.

''Course we do, or Manny wouldn't be at the school. What are you doing these days?'

'I'm meeting my sister in Calais. Are you on holiday?'

'Day trips. We like days. No more questioning now.'

'What does she want to know?' Manuel asked.

'Nothing. Nothing to do with you.'

'Is this your little girl?'

'She's fostered. I'm fostering for a friend.'

'Is Manuel fostered too?'

'What d'you mean? Certainly he is not. Manny's my boy, he's my son, little cuss. You not married then?'

'No. What happened to Al? Are you still with him?'

'He went.' I wished I hadn't asked. Her voice and her face changed. Al from Jamaica whom Tina had once loved, with whom she had lived on and off for years, running his club for him, for whom she'd do anything, had left her in the end. She used to say she'd never have a kid, that she hated them. I was glad she had Manuel to comfort her. That Manuel was part of Al whom I had known well, and liked. He'd not treated Tina well. His business was an odd one. She'd been loyal to him in her way.

'Oh Tina.'

'There we go. "Oh Tina." You ain't changed. Same posh way of speaking. "Oh Tina." I suppose you still got your head in the clouds, still a dreamer like you always was?'

'I suppose I am. People don't change a lot. You never married then?'

'Who me? I please myself.'

She looked at the children on each side of her in the queue. The lines around her eyes were still smarmed with turquoise shadow. She was beautiful still, under the paint. It was a mistake to have mentioned Al who had caused her pain, and left.

'What's your name?' I asked the little girl.

'She's Laurel. We call her Lolly,' Manuel said, tickling her neck under her hair. It was lovely to see him again, to see his teeth smiling at me.

'What are you grinning about, Manny? You behave yourself.'

'Fancy him being yours. And all the time I never knew. I've been at the school for years.'

'Why shouldn't he be? What's so strange? I used to say I'd never have one. Well I did. Here's Manny to prove it. You staying long in France?'

'Just one day, like yourself. My sister is there with her husband.'

'We like days. We never seen France yet. 'Course, we got passports.'

'I have too.'

The queue moved forward, we were going through the gate. Tina got out her cigarette case, the one I remembered, with Al written across one corner. Inside the lid was his picture, the face I remembered, like Manuel's, the same happy, smiling teeth, though Al had much darker skin. She offered me a cigarette which I refused.

'You gone health freaky in your old age?'

She'd kept her tart manner. She'd put on weight. Her plunge neckline outlined her heavy breasts. Manuel looked stuffy and uncomfortable in his heavy clothes. Laurel wore a once-white smocked dress. Her dirty socks wrinkled into her shoes, her hairslide was blue like Tina's clothes. She'd always loved turquoise blue. An oily scent hung round the three of them, like poppy juice or DDT.

'We must sit together on the train and catch up on all the news.'

'Suit yourself. I don't fancy talking. I wouldn't mind a beer. Suppose you still don't drink either?'

'I have some apples in my bag. The children might like one.'

'Don't suppose they would. We don't bother with fruit. We like chocolate for journeys. You never know what you'll pick up abroad. Chocky is safe.'

Beneath her indifference I felt that she wasn't displeased to see me. She was wary, she never had shown feelings, except for her feelings for Al.

I sat opposite the three of them in the old-fashioned carriage. The mixed smells of urine, dust and their poppy scent were strong in the stuffy air. Tina got her compact, touching the curls round her face with a spit-wetted finger. She said my own hair was better short, long hair was like a lot of seaweed hanging round. Look at Lolly, her hair was a pest. I would look better with make-up; she supposed I was too old to change. Her peach tan powder hung in the sour air as she patted her cheeks again. She emptied her bag on the seat, hunting for something.

'What's that piece of flex, Tina?'

'My tea-maker. I always bring it. You never know when we might fancy a cup. We might find ourselves where there's no tea. Here we are, chocky. Want a piece?'

Laurel let hers lie on her lap. She sat on the edge of the seat, looking at the sky above the trees. We were travelling fast. Tina nudged her. Go on eat the chocky. Laurel jumped. She looked down at her lap. She was still chewing a piece of hair. She stuffed the square of chocolate into her mouth, chewing at chocolate and hair. Tina pulled the hair out of her mouth. She shouted. Little pest. What was she, simple or somethink? Couldn't she do nothink right? Go on, eat up the chocky properly. I felt uneasy. Laurel looked frightened and pale. I asked Tina if she had more children.

'What's it to you? No. I've not.'

She ate quickly and appreciatively, not appearing to listen as I spoke about my job. I'd been saving my pay. I wanted to write a book. I'd been writing notes for years. I had brought some of my work to study on the train but I'd much rather talk to her.

'I shouldn't think writing is much cop. Is that

all you do? Cooking and writing a book? What's it about?'

She wasn't interested. I wished I hadn't told her. I remembered the old days when I'd tried telling her about my parents, how unhappy I'd felt at home. She'd only stared. I was alive, wasn't I? I had looks and health, sod anything else. Softness got no one anywhere, or brooding about the past. Grab what you could, get on the make. I'd been to a posh school. Stop moping about a mum and a dad or a married sister. I was prudish, romantic, half-baked. She'd learned her way around aged twelve, she'd learned the hard way. It was no use telling her now about my ambitions, my urge to aim high, succeed somehow, I wasn't sure yet in what field. She wouldn't understand. Instead I asked if she was happy herself, happy with the way things had turned out. She answered that she never looked back on life, nor did she whine. She believed in enjoying herself. She certainly didn't intend Manny to fill his head with dream stuff. Book writing was a waste of time.

'What work do you do now?'

'A bit of this and that. I enjoy life. I foster kids sometimes. I'm happy.'

Laurel was still quiet, watching the sky and the trees. This time she jumped so violently when I touched her knee that she wet herself. I looked down and saw her sock darken and the wet dripping from her shoe. Manuel saw before Tina did. He stood up quickly. He'd take her to the toilet, he whispered. Lolly was shy, don't blame her, she'd been too shy to speak. Laurel brought out the kindness in him. He pushed her ahead of him importantly, stamping his too-large shoes. Tina took some more chocolate. She'd taken Lolly in to help out a friend. She'd fancied a rest from fostering, only Manny had begged. He was fond of the kid, who was a nervy little beast. They all settled in the end. Her friend was in hospital.

'Do you like minding strange children? Are you fond of kids since you had Manuel?'

'Fond? I foster because it pays. I do what I please with myself.'

She swallowed some more of the chocolate. Other women of her age might look ugly, eating with an open mouth, but not Tina. I wondered how Manuel was managing and if there was soap on the train. Laurel was such a frail-looking child. I said that he seemed a particularly patient boy.

'Patient? I don't go for the love and patience stuff. I'd sooner he was tough. Dreams don't get you nowhere. Look where dreaming got you.'

She yawned, showing her chocolate-stained molars.

'Aren't you at all pleased to see me again, Tina?'

'Pleased? I don't care one way or the other. We're passing ships, that's all. I don't have no close friends. And I don't like nosey-parkers. You just remember. We ain't likely to be bumping into each other again. Kids in the home make work.'

Manuel brought Laurel back. He'd taken off her socks, she looked tidier. Her chocolatey string of hair was washed and combed. He'd cleaned her mouth and cheeks. She came and sat beside me. Her expression hadn't changed. I wanted to comfort her. I pointed to a weeping willow tree hanging over a stream, I told her to look at the birds. Some magpies were flirting their upraised tails. Some crows and two blackbirds were flying over the trees. She showed no interest, her face was quiet and blank.

'We come for a day in France, not a nature lecture. Kids don't want trees and birds, they're not at school now, you know. They've come for a spin on the train and a bit of a ride on the boat. I'd like to see France, though I've heard it's a dirty place.'

'I don't know what it's like, I've never been either. My sister Zee goes every year to the same hotel. She says that her husband is ill, so she asked me to come.'

I didn't want to lose her now that I'd found her, not until I found out what had happened in the dingy upstairs flat in Ladbroke Grove. If I was patient she'd tell me of her own accord. I asked where she was living, if she had a flat or a house.

'Maisonette. Al and I rented it before . . . I mean after Manuel was born.'

'What happened then?'

'What happened? I told you. He closed up the club. He went. Satisfied? Heard all you want to hear?'

'I'm sorry.'

I didn't like upsetting her. Her face showed pain again, a pain caused by Al who had left for good.

She tweaked another curl, she looked me straight in the face. The past was dead. Over. She never brooded or whined. Understood?

I told her about my trip to Madam Bleach who owned elderly goldfish and who had cut my hair. I told her about my boots. I clicked my earrings from side to side. Did she like them? She was more friendly by the time we reached Dover. She didn't want to touch on the past, particularly not Al. She quite liked orange scent. She told me about her poppy oil. She got it from a stall at Shepherd's Bush market, where she also bought the coloured pastes for her eyes: Indian stuff in small pots.

It was a calm crossing. Manuel and Laurel stood side by side, watching the pale, quiet sea.

Six

I was afraid of what Zee would say when she saw me arrive with Tina and two children, particularly as one of them was Manuel whom she disliked. Perhaps she wouldn't recognize him, dressed now in broadcloth and heavy shoes, with Laurel in his care. Tina came down the gangplank with her old swagger. A few beers on the boat had relaxed her. The heel-straps of her silver sandals had loosened, one of the buckles clicked against her anklet chain. From the back she would still pass as young, she'd have confidence till she died. Her poppy smell was strong.

Zee was in a crowd of people at the top of the ramp. I heard her before I caught sight of her. She wore slacks now, tight over her thighs, and a black scarf like a peasant. Her eyes were wet with tears.

'Ted isn't dead, is he? Stop making that noise, Zee.'

She shook her head.

'Is he worse?'

'He's . . . oh, Shirley.'

'Speak. What?'

'He's . . . all right.'

'You mean he isn't ill?'

'I was afraid you wouldn't come. The boat is late. I was scared.'

'Do take off that scarf. When I saw you in black I thought Ted must be dead.'

She was attracting attention by her noise. The mother of an Irish family near to us crossed herself. A child tittered. Zee hunched her shoulders, trying to calm down. She mopped her face with a small hanky. I insisted that she take off her scarf. I saw why she'd been wearing it. She'd been experimenting with curlers and dye; her hair exploded from under the scarf in a strange two-coloured burst. It practically crackled. The ends were a fizzed chocolate brown, the rest looked like singed featheres. She had humbled herself into competing with me, because Ted had liked my hair. I had to look away. I spoke sharply. Ted was alive, wasn't he? Stop dramatizing her situation. She spoke chokingly. She'd missed me, she'd been longing for me to come. She was crying from relief. I said I couldn't always be there, couldn't always be holding her hand.

'I've been feeling so cut off. It's been *awful*. Ted's getting old.'

'I suppose you mean you feel you're getting old?'

'Oy oy. What's up? What's going on? You must be Shirl's sister, Zee. What's up, duck?'

Zee looked in disbelief at Tina. Was this creature talking to her? She recognized Manuel in his too-large suit and his shoes. What ever was going on?

'Really, Shirley, I *do* think this is too much. What is that boy doing here? Trust you to do something unsuitable.'

'Look, Shirl, is she complaining? Complaining about my boy? Pardon me, Mrs Who-ever-you-are, I'm Manuel's mother, I'm Tina, Manny's mum.'

'Zee, this is Tina. I knew her a long time ago. We met up again by chance on the journey. You already know Manuel.'

'I know him all right and I certainly don't need him. As if I haven't aggravation enough,' Zee whined.

'You calling my son aggravation? You and Shirl might have been educated posh, but you certainly got no manners.'

'Shirley, who *is* this person? Why are these children here?'

'I told you, Zee. Tina is my friend.'

Zee sniffed. She had folded her scarf. I knew that she was wishing that she hadn't taken it off. Tina's own hair, artfully curled, her blue clothes and confidence put Zee to disadvantage. She'd summed Tina up instantly. She hated what she saw. Manuel's lumpy suit, Laurel's soiled dress confirmed her opinion; a riffraff family who looked as if they had fallen off a barrow. Why did I have to involve myself with such people? I had come to rescue *her*.

Tina spoke loudly. 'You coming with us now, Shirl? We don't have a lot of time. You might as well join our party, seeing as your sister's hubby ain't ill. We're off for some French nosh. Manny wants some snails. Coming?'

'And wine,' Manuel murmured.

I told Tina that I couldn't. I'd like to have come; I had to stay with Zee. I had promised. Zee said loudly that if that was the case, Ted was waiting.

'Pardon me, don't let me stop you. I can see we're not wanted. Come on, Manny. We ain't good enough for these two. Posh couple of cows.'

'Oh don't take offence, Tina.'

'I said posh cows and I meant it.'

Zee pulled her shoulders back, speaking carefully with her best accent. 'Look here, my good woman, I don't know who you are but a taxi is waiting to take us to Le Grand. I am sorry you are feeling strange, you are probably not used to France. I am sorry Shirley can't help you, nor can she join your party.'

She was in charge again, had the situation in hand. She had got me over to France. Now she had shown Tina her place. She shook out her scarf, reknotting it under her chin. This market woman with the brassy hair and squalid offspring wasn't worth getting upset over.

Tina lost her temper. She shouted at Zee.

'Don't try and come the madam with me. There's not an inch of London I don't know, plus all the seasides around. We can look after ourselves a lot better than you can, seemingly. You can't breathe without screaming for Shirl. We can manage ourselves. And Manny my son speaks French.'

'*Indeed*? Your son? Ah yes.'

Zee looked at Manuel's dark face, his hair, his clothes, his shoes. She looked at Tina's bare third finger. If she had her way she'd run every black from the country, and every half-caste too. Tina put England to shame.

I wished that they'd never met. They brought out the worst in each other. I was ashamed of them both. I would much rather have joined Tina now, in search of snails, rude postcards and wine, instead of going with Zee to their staid hotel. Tina was deeply hurt, she left without speaking again, swaggering her hips, her shoe-buckle clicking at her anklet chain. Manuel looked back yearningly, as he had when he'd left my flat.

'Pathetic. A travesty of a family,' Zee said loudly. 'Some persons shouldn't be allowed children, there ought to be a law.'

I stared after Tina's back. I hadn't got her address. I'd found her and I'd lost her. I wanted to call her, I wanted to see her again. I felt that I'd come here for nothing. Zee had made a fool of me, Ted wasn't dying. Tina had taken offence. I wished that I hadn't come.

'Shut up, Zee.'

'I suppose she's another of your secrets? That

hidden past of yours?'

'She was a good friend once. I used to like her a lot. The little girl is fostered, she's fostering her for a friend. Tina has character and guts. Is the hotel far away?'

Zee walked ahead of me to the taxi; contemptuous, curious, ashamed.

The weather on the other side of the channel was wetter, cooler, darker. The sky was dark grey. The taxi driver was half asleep at his wheel. One elbow rested against his open window, his cheek rested on his palm. He wore his beret tipped over his eyes and chewed a matchstick. His face didn't change as we got into the back. He drove the clientele to and from the Le Grand regularly. As we moved off the Irish family stared after us. The mother shook her head. Our driver drove fast, hooting, taking sharp corners, his cheek still against his palm. The suburbs here were like the suburbs of Brighton, the only French-looking person was the driver. The pedestrians, the cyclists and other drivers all looked English, but slow-moving and tired, as if they were waiting to die. There was no holiday atmosphere. Zee liked this end of Calais because it was English and quiet. Few trippers penetrated the streets round the Le Grand, few radios were played, it could be a corner of England, and English was spoken in most of the shops, Zee told me. She and Ted liked the manager of the hotel and his English wife.

We turned into a crescent-shaped drive, bordered with palm trees. More of the palms grew on either side of the double doorway. Le Grand was woven in black into the doormat. I wiped my new red boots. Inside, the lobby was dark; there was a musty smell. The polished panelling, the dark red wallpaper and the lighting made it feel like a church. There were palms under the chandelier that glittered above the stairs. No one was behind the desk. Zee got her own key from its hook. She was restored to her normal self now she was back at the Le Grand and could show me where to go. Quiet voices sounded from the dining-room behind the stairway. I followed her down a passage. She stopped at a dark brown door.

'She's here. She's come. Shirley has come at last.'

The room was as I'd imagined. There was the oak table separating the twin beds. There were the folded dressing-gowns, the slippers, Zee's clock, Ted's folded *Times*. And Ted, lying in one of the beds, was laughing at me. He looked better than I'd seen him look for years. His cheeks had a tinge of colour, his eyelids were less drawn. His Adam's apple glowed between the starched points of his pyjama collar. He'd played a successful trick.

'You aren't ill at all, Ted. You got me here on a hoax.'

'Don't be hard on us, my dear. My doctor did advise me to rest more. I was tired when I got here. I've improved. Your arrival completes the cure.'

He stretched his hand out. I ignored it. I'd been cheated; I turned to Zee who was by the dressing-table, fussing again with her scarf.

'You're despicable.'

'But you came, Shirley. You're here. Can't you just enjoy it?' Her eyes pleaded again from under the chocolate frizz.

'Forget? You've lied to me. I've put myself out for you. My plans . . .'

'Ah, the famous plans. If you weren't so secretive I might understand you more. You don't understand *me*. I've been lonely. There's nothing to do.'

'You knew what it was like. Why come here if you don't like it? You tricked me.'

Her eyes went sulky. She combed her chocolate hair. Wisps fell to the floor as the teeth rasped through the frizzy ends. I looked down at the black and brown scraps. I ought to leave at once. Tina wouldn't have allowed herself to be duped, she'd have walked out. I couldn't. Zee needed me, she had power. I looked round at the room, at the half-drawn blinds, the chandelier, the chair like a commode by the bed. The room had a tainted feel. Above Ted's head was a picture of a child, stretching out dingy hands. Above the other bed was a flock of birds. Both paintings were dark with age. Nothing about the room pleased me. Instead of a sick man I had found a healthy fraud.

'But you will stay, Shirley? Dear sister-in-law, stay for my sake, as well as Zee's.'

Honestly, Ted, why did you come here? It's not even very clean. You, Zee, of all people.'

She was so neat, so houseproud at home. She

polished ashtrays, she vacuumed, each cushion was plumped and placed. I supposed they had chosen this decayed hotel because of its familiarity. They knew what to expect. As you got older the unexpected was frightening. Ted was old. It was getting late. I felt tired. I said I would stay for one night.

'We booked you a room. We guessed you'd stay. We booked you the room next door. When you see it you'll feel differently. I admit the rooms are small. Look, we can go this way, through our balcony. Our balconies adjoin.'

The windows opened on to a square walled area with a rusty table, some chairs and a brown umbrella for use in sunny weather. Now the chair seats were puddled with rain. Zee pushed the chairs out of the way to climb the adjoining wall. It was easy. Follow her.

'This one is yours. Come on. Your room is the same as ours. There's a shower. It's all on us. You can stay till the end of the month.'

Her eyes pleaded again but I was firm. One night, no more. I wished I could feel fonder of her, that we could be closer than we were. She tried to govern, at the same time she tried to cling. Poor Ted, who would do anything for her, got no thanks.

The shabby balconies pleased me more than the rooms. You could lean over the parapet to the garden, where a few flowers hung their heads round the edge of a waterlogged lawn. It could be any garden anywhere, neat without being tended.

The plants needed staking. There was no sea in sight. I asked Zee about the other guests.

'Look. Over there. There are some of them. We keep ourselves to ourselves.'

At one side of the lawn was a grey awning stretched over some canvas chairs. A few old people huddled there, waiting for the rain to stop. Their greyish clothing blended with the sky and the grey awning; they were easy to overlook. They sat like stone people, with bags or sticks in their hands, as if they'd been there for years. Zee said that they seemed older that summer. The same people came every year. This year their ages showed. It frightened her. She'd telephoned me to come on the spur of the moment. Oh if only I would stay.

'It's all much shabbier than I'd expected. I'd expected it to be quiet.'

'There's a swimming pool. Over there. No one uses it. You could go swimming now.'

I could see a corner of grey water surrounded by more grey tiles and canvas chairs. I was tired. I had no costume. It was so empty. No sea front, no traffic and hardly any guests.

'It *is* quiet. You can see why I needed you.'

'You have Ted. He needs you and he's getting old. They're all old here. Are you scared of getting old?'

She flushed. She said of course she wasn't. And I shouldn't be taken in by Ted. He might appear considerate, he really was quite selfish. I thought how spoiled she was. Touching her chocolate hair again she asked who Tina was. When had I known her before?

'I told you. Ages ago. When I first left home. You were married, it was awful, I needed a friend. Tina was good to me. I'm pleased to meet her again.'

'It's a pity you didn't do better at school. Or some kind of training.'

'You didn't.'

'But I'm married. I don't understand what you see in her. What's she doing with that Negro child? She looks no better than a . . .'

'He's half West Indian. I knew his father. Tina loved the father very much. And she was my friend.'

I didn't want to shock or distress her by telling her more than that. She said that the other child, the white one didn't look all there.

'I want to see Tina again. I used to like her. I still do.'

I thought I was hungry until I saw the food. I went to the dining-room with Zee and watched her eat steamed fish, butter beans. She ate my portion when she had finished hers, spitting the bones neatly, wiping the white plate clean. The Le Grand was the most depressing place I'd ever been in. I kept wondering about Tina. I left Zee and went to my room. I piled the pillow and quilt from the second bed on to mine. I'm fond of deep daytime sleep and heavy bedding. I wished I could wake up in London without the struggle of getting there. I hadn't seen or heard anything that

I liked yet in France. The wet weather made everything damp and cold to touch, the bed-clothes smelled of mice. Outside on the balcony the rain beat on the red tiles. I was still tired when I woke up. The water in the shower, which was a kind of cupboard in the corner, took a long time to heat. I longed for my own large bath, my airy window over the fire escape, my mirror and scented soaps. The shower recess was dark, the shower rail had rusted black from a row of wire coat-hangers. The shower curtains were torn. Before I could wash I had to pull a plug of soap-scummed hair from the drain. Lukewarm water fell on me at last. The soap was transparent with use, but the small hotel towel, though marked with iron mould, was clean. Soon I'd be home, soon I'd be out of the Le Grand. I spun round my bed, my skirt flared out like a petal. I rubbed up my boots with my towel. The rain had stopped. I leaned over the parapet again. The lawn was empty now, the elderly guests had gone into change for the evening meal. I climbed over and walked across the muddy wet grass to the pool. Leaves floated on the surface. I tested the water, it felt very cold. It was a long thin pool, quite deep at one end. I longed for the sun, for colours, birds, young people and tasty food.

Ted joined Zee and me for dinner. He breathed a little fast, leaning on his stick, but he looked fresh and fit, happy to see me there.

'Welcome to the Le Grand cuisine Shirley. The fare may not be imaginative, but plain English

sitting near her timidly stretched out his glass. Tina obliged. She kissed her plum-passioned finger-tips, laying them to his lips. He trembled, the others thrilled. What an ill-bred woman. Those shoes, that ankle jewellery, those tipsy-looking eyes. Delightful, they couldn't look hard enough. Disgusting, that blouse, that paint. Her shouts would stay etched in their memories. The old gentleman nodded, shivering with joy. How he agreed with Tina on the subject of snail-eating, and those dreadful-smelling cheeses. He looked away when she spoke about French toilets. You could see people's feet outside in the street. The French didn't allow you the privacy to be excused. Men ogled you in a dirty-minded way. They muttered things she didn't understand, touching their zips, not like England. France was a dirty nation, eating dirty food, them and their dirty talk. They drove on the wrong side, too. Ted leaned forwards, captivated. Such frank talk was refreshment. When she'd dealt with French habits she started on men in general. She was qualified to talk. She drained her glass, holding it out to Ted. Talking made her dry. Yes, men were her business, had been for many years, she was an expert judge, could tell what a man liked in a wink, how he'd behave when he got it. Love was her business, she provided the goods, men paid. Got it?

The elderly gentleman blushed. Expressions round the room tightened, jawlines were raised, elderly ears strained. They ought to leave. They couldn't. What did the woman mean? What could she be referring to? She ought to be shown the door. Shocking. Exciting. She was obscene. She ought to come every year. In the future, over knitting and newspapers, the elderly ones would recall this holiday supper when a woman with a black child spoke of unmentionable goings on. They'd think of France, they'd think of Tina. Secretly they might even wish they'd been a bit like her, with a bit of her spirit and zest. Her black child lowered the tone of the Le Grand. The white one should be in bed. Dirty painted person.

Being with Zee and Tina at the same time was a strain. Divided in loyalty I felt pulled two ways. I liked Tina, though she revived a time I wanted to forget. I was sorry for my sister, trying not to cry from humiliation. Tina leaned back, her blue blouse a spot of colour in the drabness of the room. She waved her glass, she shouted. The rest of the table were silent. Manuel and Laurel serenely shared a plate of food, disassociating themselves as if used to Tina's ways. Zee stared into her lap. No one noticed me leave. I went to my room and slept until morning.

When I woke I heard splashing. I couldn't think where I was. Of course, the Le Grand, with Tina one side of me, my sister Zee the other. I had slept the night in my clothes, my red skirt was creased. Someone was outside in the pool. I looked. I could make out a dark head moving up and down and a small figure by the edge of the pool. It was Manuel demonstrating to Laurel. He got out and jumped in again with a splash.

'Come out, Manuel. It isn't five o'clock. You'll wake the people.'

He took no notice, continuing to swim up and down.

'Laurel. Lo-llee. Tell Manny that's enough. He's making too much noise.'

She didn't look round.

The French doors on my left opened.

'Who do you think you're shouting at, Shirl? They ain't your kids. You woke me up with your bawling.'

'They woke *me* up. It's much too early for them to be outside.'

'Who says? I let them. I said they could. It's our trip, don't interfere.'

'They'll wake up the old people. All that puffing and splashing. Why does he breathe so hard?'

'Don't ask me. You know what Manny's like where water is concerned. It won't harm the old freaks, too much sleeping is bad when you're old.'

'Are you all right, Tina?'

''Course. I see you slept in your clothes. We didn't have no change either.'

She stood on her side of the balcony wall, wearing her slip. Without her bra her figure flopped. She had a stale smell under her poppy oil and her toes were grimy in the dawning light. Compared with Zee, whom I'd never seen dirty and who went to bed powdered and scrubbed inside a buttoned nightgown, Tina was a slut. But washed or unwashed, drunk or sober, Tina had style. She'd draw eyes, make herself noticed until the day she died. I wouldn't mention last night in the dining-room, I wanted her to go on being friendly. I confided in her.

'I don't like this place, Tina. I didn't want to stay. Zee tricked me. Ted isn't ill, she wanted to get me here.'

'This place is all right, not like the rest of France. I don't object to here. What's wrong with Zee, why is she spineless? Why can't she manage without you?'

'She's been like that a long time. She's spoilt, We were close when we were young, we planned to be together when we grew up. She changed. I changed too. I want to leave after breakfast, get back to London.'

'Ted's okay. She's a bleeding misery. D'you fancy a cup of tea?'

'We can't order yet. It's too early.'

'I've got my tea-maker. Remember? I never travel without. Come in my room, we'll have a brew up. I'll plug it into the light. Manny and Loll will like a drink presently, after they've finished their swim.'

I told her I wondered about the electricity, might it not be different in France? There was a flash. Tina stood holding the flex, the end was blackened. There was a burning smell. I switched on the bedside light. The room stayed dark.

'Oh Tina, what have you done? The power *is* different in France.'

'Trust France to be different. Awkward lot. Shit. Not to worry, though, we'll have a cold lemon. You don't catch me stranded, I've got powder. I hope the whole building ain't dark.'

'I'm afraid it might be.'

She stirred the packet of powder into the tooth glasses. She didn't care, nothing got her down, not like old Zee, poor fish. What was she, butch or somethink? Not that she cared, sex took different people different ways but Zee ought to have more guts.

I criticized Zee myself, she irritated me, I often hated her. I didn't like Tina criticizing. She was my sister, the only one I had. I said I thought she was happy in her own way with Ted. She complained a lot, it was to do with being spoiled. She was luckier than some. I refused the fizzy drink, I was afraid of the tap water in France.

Tina and I were alone for the first time since Ladbroke Grove. I felt the old closeness, dependence. She emptied her bag on the bed, hunting among her nail polish bottles, her 'Passionate Plum' and 'Purple Bruise' jars. I saw the cigarette case with Al's face in it, the face I remembered so well. I remembered how we used to collect cocktail sticks from the drinks. We got a bonus each night. I asked Tina about Pauline, what had happened to her, did she know?

'She's a loser too. I ain't got no patience with weak people. People who can't stand on their feet. She's in and out of hospital. Depressions. Shit.'

She jabbed polish onto her thumbnail. At least

I'd shown some fight. I had a job of a kind. I ought to get a bloke. Everyone needed to come first to another person. I ought to pack in being so nosey, and stop dreaming. It didn't pay to dream.

'It's not that I'm nosey, so much as curious about things I feel I should know.'

'I'd like to know when's breakfast. I fancy something hot.'

'If the main fuse has blown they won't be able to cook. There'll be nothing to eat or drink. I'd like to be out of here.'

The children came in from the pool, climbing the parapet, their feet making tracks on the tiles. They wore their underpants and sat on Tina's bed, their wet calves dangling. They drank the drink made from the lemon powder. Manuel was hungry, he said. Tina said breakfast would be late most probably, they would fill in their time with a wash. The water in their shower was cold, could they come in and use my shower? A hot shower would warm the kids up after their early swim.

They weren't interested. They would rather stay and play with Tina's bottles, preferring to dry off naturally on her bed rather than fuss with soap and towels. They didn't often get the chance to play with Tina's paints. She got huffy, her bag was private.

She walked round my room, still in her grubby slip. She examined my earrings, shaking them under her curls, she tried on my new red boots. My feet were longer and narrower. She preferred her poppy oil to the orange stuff I wore. Where had I bought that skirt? She seemed to enjoy the quiet of my room, was more relaxed when the children weren't there.

'What about Manuel and Lolly, won't they worry, Tina? Hadn't you better have your bath?'

'Suppose you're right.'

'And perhaps we ought to tell the manager about fusing the lights.'

She walked slowly to the shower cupboard. She rattled the coat hangers, pulling the curtains tightly across. I thought of my mother again when she hummed 'Bye Bye Blackbird'. I wished Zee and I hadn't been ashamed of her, wished we'd been kinder, wished that I'd known her better. 'Make my bed and light the light, I'll be home late tonight, Bye bye blackbird.' Tina called out that she didn't like the soap. Dirty nation, not used to soaping themselves. She looked young and sweet when she came out again, with the towel wrapped round her head. She must have been a pretty child. I asked her if she wished life had treated her differently, or if she had a future dream.

'You and your dreams. I face life as it is. Can I borrow your earrings?'

'The hooks are difficult to manage, you'll have to look in a glass. My God, Tina, have you been hurt? What's that under your slip? It looks like a bruise.'

I made her show me. From her navel to her pubic bone and stretching from hip to hip were navy and black weals. She was sulky when I questioned.

'I fell.'

'Those didn't come from a fall. You've been hit, beaten up. Who by, Tina?'

'Oh don't, Shirl. Stop making a fuss.'

'Tell me. I must know.'

'My bloke. Shit, Shirl, stop being nosey. He's got a temper, if you want to know. It's nothing.'

'Not your regular boyfriend? It looks agonizing.'

'I need him. I'm fond of him.'

'Fond? He did that and you're fond? Who is he?'

'What's it to do with you? Nosey-parkering again? If I don't care, why should you?

'Please, Tina. What's been happening? I'm worried.'

I had never seen her cry. She made no sound. Tears dripped from her chin. I begged her to tell me. She turned her head away.

'I'm sick of it. What shall I do? Oh Lor'.'

From the passage we heard exclamations and orders. Feet hurried by, light switches were snapped on and off. The manager's voice was angry.

'Mum, when is breakfast?' Manuel called.

Tina went on crying. It was my suggestion that we leave at once. Zee didn't need me, Tina did. By the time Zee and Ted realized I'd gone I'd be on the ferry boat again, away from the Le Grand for good.

Eight

I rang the bell at the reception desk. No one came. The rows of keys hanging behind it could hardly be seen in the gloom. The chandelier was dark. Through the light from the double doorway you could just make out the welcome notice hanging over the desk. 'Welcome to the Le Grand. English cooking a speciality.' Behind the stairway, from the dining-room came raised voices. At last the English manageress came, her angel sleeves rolled back, her face still pained and pinched. She stared at the blackened flex still hanging from Tina's bag. Before she could say anything Tina said, 'Bill please. We can't stop in the dark. We're off. D'you get many power cuts in France?'

The manageress obeyed, her lips were thin while she wrote. Excitement in the dining-room late last night. The elderly guests upset, no lighting this morning, all due to the red-haired hussy. She wasn't sorry to see the back of us.

'Posh cow,' Tina said.

The taxi with the same driver took us away, tearing out of the crescent-shaped drive with squealing tyres, his hand still supporting his cheek. He spat out his toothpick when he saw Tina, his eyes going hard and bright. Tina, once out of sight of the Le Grand, had gone sullen and quiet. Our closeness was broken, she regretted confiding. I had told her that her wound might go septic, it should have proper care. She'd looked furious. She snapped at the driver.

'Look, mister, eyes on the job, not on me. Look at the road.'

'*Madame*? *Excusez-moi*?'

'Never mind the "excusy-mois". Let's go if we've got to.'

She had almost tripped on the flex as she got into the cab. Her sandal straps still trailed.

'Thank goodness that's over. What an awful place,' I sighed.

Tina had obviously enjoyed the Le Grand although it was in France. She'd have liked to have stayed, but not with Zee, a killjoy and a cow. Zee was worse than the French.

'Look out, mister, can't you drive on the proper side?'

'*Madame?*'

'Can't you do nothing right? French pigs. I want to get back whole.'

'Don't, Tina, he might understand.'

'So what? My head aches. I feel sick.'

I told her I'd get something on the boat for her,

I'd look after her.

'Don't try and latch on to me. We won't be seeing each other no more, not after this we won't.'

Manuel looked sorrowful. I had tried to wipe the lipstick off his cheeks, traces were still round his eyes. He'd drawn thick black eyebrows over his own with mascara. 'Passionate Plum' polish had spilled over Laurel's socks. They'd enjoyed themselves until I had made them stop. Fate had brought Tina and I together, I couldn't just let her and the children go without a fight, not now.

'At least let me help with the children on the boat. While you lie down somewhere.'

'Suit yourself. If I feel like a laydown I will. I get a lot of heads.'

'The sun is coming out. I hope it stays nice for the crossing. Look Laurel, the clouds are like birds. Can you see?'

'Oh leave the kid alone. You and your clouds and birds.'

Once on board, Tina made for a seat, kicking her silvery sandals under it, lying on her back, with her coat bunched over her stomach. She groaned, closing her eyes, heedless of the crew's shouting, the loading and unloading of freight, the crashing of luggage being pulled along the decks. A few of the passengers stared. The two children smeared with lipstrick, neglected and oddly dressed, the worn and lovely woman lying on her back were worth looking at. Tugs hooted, sea birds called through the salty air. There was a smell of rope.

'Shall we walk about while your Mum rests? We'll explore. Come on, Lolly.'

'She isn't Lolly's Mum. Lolly's Mum is in hospital.'

'I know. Tina told me. What a lot of seagulls. What a noise they make.'

Lolly went on sucking a piece of hair, ignoring the clouds and birds. I asked if they'd like something to eat. Manuel insisted that they only ate chocolate when travelling but I bought coffee in plastic cups, soft rolls with egg in them and triangular pieces of cheese in foil wrappings. Lolly ran to Tina, shaking her by the arm. Tina swore and groaned, turning her head away. There was a slight swell. I asked Manuel if he knew that Tina had a sore stomach, had she said anything? Did he know what had happened? He looked up at the seagulls that screamed around the boat. 'Long ago. Long ago.' He tangled and untangled his fingers. I told him that I used to know Tina very well, long ago, that I worried about her now. It was wrong to cross-question him, the sweat showed on his lip. I didn't say anything more.

The expanse of water between the boat and the quay widened. The waves were dotted with birds. Look out, don't let Lolly lean over, I warned. Danger was everywhere, in tap water, swimming pools and sea. The worst dangers were the cruelties that people inflicted on each other. I longed to ask Manuel about the attendant at the pool, how well he knew him. I hated it when he twisted and tangled his hands.

The birds went on calling. 'Long ago, long ago', their beaks widening and closing in the salty air. I threw some of the rolls, which no one wanted, watching the birds swoop and sweep to catch the pieces before they fell in the sea. Both of the children seemed tense. Lolly flung a small crust but it only fell at her feet.

'What's going on over there?' Tina called. 'You been asking nosey questions again?'

'I'm just trying to keep them happy. I want you to rest. I'm keeping them amused.'

'I don't trust you, you want too much. "Do you remember?" "What happened?" "Are you happy?" It's nothing to do with you. Life ain't perfect, you know. You got a lot to learn. You ain't perfect.'

'I know. And nor are you.'

'At least I got my kid.'

'I had one too once. Remember? What happened to it? That's all I really want to know.'

'I didn't want to meet you. Far as I'm concerned when we hit Dover that's it. Ta ta. Cheerio. Chow.' She closed her eyes as if her burst of anger weakened her. She covered her eyes. Shit.

Laurel ran to her again, touching her face. Tina swore. She aimed a blow. Keep off, pest.

'Don't hit her, Tina.'

'It's no concern of yours what I do.'

'Children do concern me. I work with them. I don't like them getting hit. Laurel's unhappy.'

'Unhappy? Lolly's a lucky child.'

'She's too quiet. She doesn't speak or smile

enough.'

Tina said she supposed I'd be threatening her with the cruelty man next. Loll was fine and there was nothing she didn't know about kids. I wished that I hadn't seen her stomach. It changed things and made me worried. I wanted the children's trust. I wanted to protect them.

I took their hands getting off the boat. We were the first on land, the first to board the train. Tina came after, her coat dragging, trailing her blackened flex. The carriage smelled the same. I determined that I'd get the children engrossed, absorb them in a game so that they'd like me. What games did they like? Noughts and crosses? Paper darts? Drawing? I reached in my bag for my notes.

Manuel explained that they liked making paper cutouts. You made holes and patterns with scissors when the paper was folded. Or you could just tear. When the paper was opened you had a nice pattern.

'I know. I remember. I used to make them. Lace traycloths and napkins.'

The paper tore easily. They folded, they poked, they tore. Pieces of my future book were scattered over the floor.

'Look, miss. Look what I made.'

'Don't call me miss, Manuel. I'm Shirley, or Shirl if you like that better.'

Laurel bent low over her work, the tip of her tongue moved as she worked. Soon the red seat was covered with small lacey cloths. She was a pretty child when she was happy, with pretty teeth and honey-coloured eyes. I asked Manuel if they would both like to visit me in my home, would he bring Lolly if Tina allowed?

'To see that parrot what lives in your building? Could we go swimming too? I want to learn Lolly to swim before she goes back to her Mum. I must learn her.'

'Not at the old pool. The new one, the other side of the bridge. The new pool is larger. Yes, we'll go.'

'Will you write, miss? Shirley, I mean. Write a letter to ask us?'

As the train drew in I bent to pick up the paper. Tina pulled the children out quickly. She didn't speak, she'd hadn't spoken a word on the train. She didn't wave or look back, but hurried them away. I called. I ran after them. I tripped over suitcases, I stumbled into a child. I saw her go through the barrier, I lost her in the crowds. Tina. Tin–a. There she was, putting her hand out for a taxi. I didn't know her address.

Nine

I felt that they needed me. I had less interest now in the whereabouts of the baby I'd once had. Nameless, faceless, sexless it had faded into second place. Manuel and Laurel had been happy, folding and tearing my notes on the Dover/Victoria train, and wanted to see me again, they wanted me to write to them. I didn't even know Tina's surname now, much less the address. I couldn't find out at the school, term didn't start for five weeks. One minute Tina had been asleep, the next minute she was off. The paper that I hadn't gathered up from the train fluttered out of the carriage and down the platform in the faint hot breeze. I had no regrets about my notes. Tina needed me, so did the children. I'd let them get away.

The streets outside the station were filled with flying ants. England felt closer, hotter, damper than France. I felt an ant on my neck, another crawled over my wrist. I swatted it and missed. Where had the children gone?

It was dark inside the hall of my building, the stairway bulb had blown. I felt for the bottom tread, for the newel post on my right. The stair rail was sticky with heat. I had left one dark hallway, here was another, and my building hadn't burned down or been flooded. I would let Mr Caige know I was back.

'Hello. I've just got back from France.'

'M-m-m-miss Shirley. I have m-m-missed you.'

He stuttered when he was pleased, especially with his m's. Nearsightedness and deafness made him shy. He was a natural recluse, he had his parrot but few human contacts. He kept our landing tidy, shooing away intruders. They often stole the electric light bulb. Our front doors were on either side of the stairs. I spoke slowly in short sentences, looking into his face. He had a trick of dropping his teeth, to rest them on his tongue.

'I've been to Calais.'

'Ballet? I had a weakness for terpsichorian art. Long ago.'

'Calais. For one day.'

'Ballet on Monday? I will escort you there, with your permission.'

He put out his hand invitingly, quirking his fingers. He bowed. I shook my head. I didn't stay to explain, I didn't want to embarrass him.

My flat was as I had left it, except for an invasion of flies. The onions in the vegetable rack had rotted.

The apples in the fruit bowl had brown cavities in their bright green skins. The flies hovered lovingly. I opened the kitchen window and more flies flew in and some flying ants. I flapped a cloth at them. I unbolted the bathroom window. I flapped a second cloth. Outside, the lane was quiet except for hammering from the repair shop at the far end. I leaned out further and a bird flew in, hitting my cheek as it passed. I don't like feathers touching me, I hit at it with the cloth. Its wings fanned me. I hit harder. I've always had a fear of birds coming near my hair. I love watching them, I don't like them coming close. It swooped again, its claws scratching my fringe. Birds have vermin in the scales of their legs. I beat at it, I shouted. Get away. Get out, don't come near. It is falling into the bath. I see it panting, I see its heart beating. Get out, get away, don't come near. It's up again. Bastard. Spy. My hair, keep away from my hair. It's down the toilet bowl, flapping. I hope it breaks its beak. There. Now, got you, up under the porcelain rim. Hold it, cupped in your hands. Wet wings, slippery and black. Sit it on the table by the rotting fruit. Birds like fruit. Eat some, be my guest.

I'd saved it, I watched it gasp. I felt no pity, only dislike. I wanted it to go. The bell rang.

'M-m-miss Shirley. Here is your m-m-milk. But you are agitated. *Molto agitato*. Can I help?'

'A bird came.'

'Word game? What game? I used to do crosswords once. Dear me, look at that, a blackbird.

Half-drowned-looking. Afflicted songster.'

The bird sat near the apples, breast panting. Mr Caige put out his hand, his expression sad and kind. He leaned over, nearly toppling, righting himself again. He had mentioned his dizzy spells. Old age got you, you couldn't beat old time. This songster was young yet, time for more singing, more flight.

'Oh let me persuade you songster, to take wing again, fly.' He moved round the table intoning his song, trying to get me to smile. 'She went to Calais and not a ballet, to see a bird and speak the word.'

The bird shifted, moving in feathery jerks. It tried to rise, to fly, then fell back and died. The flies went on hovering, the ants crawled with lopsided wings, the blackbird lay on it's side, a bunch of black feathers and two verminous legs. Mr Caige looked like a sad elderly bird himself, standing and watching the bird. He had a kinship with feathered life, his parrot was his friend. Parrots had long lives, small English birds did not. Look at the flies, they were mourning. He started to mime grief with an excess of feeling. He waved his handkerchief, he dropped his false top teeth.

'A dead bird indoors is bad luck.' I said.

'Do not distress yourself M-m-m-miss Shirley. I did the best I could. Had it been a word and not a bird, the outcome might have been different.'

He would dispose of the remains with fitting ceremony, that's if I would permit? I said I couldn't touch it. Did birds really have lice on them?

He fetched toilet paper from the bathroom, wrapping the corpse in pink. 'Rest in peace,' he murmured, flushing the dead bird away. He washed his hands with my new soap, drying himself with care.

'Pardon the enquiry but have you drain trouble?'

'It's the onions.'

'Bunions?'

He looked doubtfully at his toe, pushed sideways under the suede slipper. He was happy to have helped. Yes, he would appreciate some tea. I gave him the top of the milk, I knew he liked it. I wanted to tell him about Tina, about her son Manuel and the little girl she was fostering. I wanted advice, I didn't want to shout. He had no idea that I'd ever worked in a nightclub, that I'd once had a child, that I'd known sorrow and despair. He didn't even know about Zee and our arguments.

'M-m-m-miss Shirley, you are a consolation in my quiet life.'

'You don't have to call me miss. You help me as well.'

'Shirley then, if you will permit. My own name is Cyrus. Cyrus Caige.'

He bent over my hand. Long ago he'd been a librarian. He'd no idea that I had thoughts about writing a book to help me remodel my life. Perhaps he had some idea of my past shame and guilt because once he had whispered that if he had one maxim to guide him it was to have a high self-regard.

When he had left I threw out the fruit and vegetables, I wiped the sills clean of dead ants. Where were Tina and the two children? What were they doing now? I must stop thinking about them. Manuel knew where I lived, he'd come if he wanted. I had planned to teach him to cook. Rewriting the notes that the two of them had used for paper traycloths would take up a lot of time. I must stop thinking about that dying bird. There was no sound from Cyrus Caige. The hammering in the back lane had stopped. I checked that the window was locked. I was safe, I was alone, I'd got what I wanted. I wanted the children again. They weren't my children, they were Tina's, nothing to do with me. She was right, I shouldn't interfere. Except that she'd been in a fight, they might be endangered.

I was almost asleep when my earlobes started to throb. My glittery red earrings had torn my flesh after sleeping in them in France. I had to use hot water and soap to get them out. My earlobes started to bleed. Caring for these small sores made me forget everything else.

Ten

My fine skin marks easily. The throbbing in my earlobes came in waves. The stuffy room made it difficult to breathe. My earlobes were bleeding again. I got up. I leaned across the sink in the bathroom to look at them again. I don't mind the sight of my own blood. A few drops fell on to my neck. I bathed and swabbed the small wounds. My period was due. Perhaps it was best that Tina had given me the slip at Victoria. There was before Ladbroke Grove and after. I didn't miss the old life, I missed friendship.

I would get up early and make a special breakfast of pancakes with chopped nuts, anchovies and honey. My decision to swim one last time at the old pool wasn't to do with Manuel or the hope that I might see him there, not consciously. I wanted to go once more to the place where I'd been happy. From now on I'd go to the new pool. During the night I had decided to put the Le

Grand episode out of my mind. I couldn't put the clock back. I had changed. Tina had changed. She was right, they weren't my business. I longed to have water over, round and under me. At the old pool one more time.

The street was empty still except for the milkman crashing bottles in the doorways. The flying ants were gone. My earlobes still hurt but had stopped bleeding. I wore the skirt again. At the traffic lights you could still see the stain Zee had made when she'd been ill in the road. A pigeon pecked near it. I hoped that she'd stay in France until I'd got over seeing Tina. When she came back I'd be kinder to her, for my sake as well as hers. I'd try to be a friend as well as a better sister.

The black youths hadn't gathered yet on the steps of the old swimming pool. The building looked empty, with a closed, sealed look. The double doors opened when I pushed and there was the cashier counting her money before locking her old-fashioned till. There was the chlorine smell, but fainter. Her cold fingers took my money. There were the beetles again.

'Hullo, miss. Come to see me?'

'You said you were leaving. I didn't know you'd be here.'

'Boss asked me to stay. Sickness. There's a lot of sickness about. Sorry, darling. I'm here alrighty.'

'It's of no interest to me whether you're here or not.'

His whispering voice, his teeth, his curious whitish hair made me shiver. How could I have forgotten? I would treat him as Zee would, as a paid servant, a no one. His job was to man the pool, sweep up insects, see to the drains. I'd keep my mind on my swim as I walked to my cubicle. I'd pretend he wasn't there. Shut the door quickly. Oh Zee, where are you now?

In my hurry I'd forgotten to put on my costume under my tiered skirt. I didn't care, I'd swim in my bra and pants. It was early, there were no other swimmers yet. 'Darling.' He'd said, 'Darling.' Impertinent man. No one could touch me. Prowler. Peeping tom. Bastard. He's standing outside my door. I'm frightened of loud breathing. Noise, cruel eyes won't hurt me, pull the green canvas flap tighter, I shall never be here again. I shall never put my clothes on that cracked seat again, nor smell talcum and stale knickers. No more corn plasters stained with blood. I've been happy here. I'm moving on. Paid servant. Cleaner. Cheat. I can see part of his cheek between the door and the jamb. He's whispering again.

'I didn't mean to scare you, darling. Beg pardoney a lot. I want to be your friend and there's something I must say.'

Say nothing. Don't answer. I'm scared.

'Look, miss, I've been patient. Don't get high horsey with me.'

I'm not afraid of him. He's mad. Pull down my bra, pull up my briefs, the crotch of my briefs is damp. My period beginning on time. Doesn't show. That madman won't stop me going in, nor will a speck of blood. His canvas shoes show underneath my door. His eyes make me blush inside. Men watching you, men undressing you, men wondering if you will. It shows in their eyes. ('Hullo, darling, will you be friendly?' 'Do you fraternize after hours?' 'I'm lonely, dream eyes, I need a friend.') I have changed. I have grown. I am free. I'm not that girl any more. I never was inside. Not that life, never again. I'll open the door now.

Jump. Cold water. Down. Swim downwards, push with your arms, push downwards away from harm. I'm on the bottom, rough tiling is scratching my palms. I'm safe here, away from harm, I'm on the floor of the pool with dead insects for company and a forgotten coin. But I must have air. Must . . . breathe . . . I . . . don't . . . want . . . to . . . drown. Dying is lonely, I must have air. Up . . . up . . . bubbles in my ears. He's there, he's near, he's in the water now. His pale eyes are peering, his ash-coloured hair is wet. His eyes, wet teeth, his hands. I must get away from his hands. Touching me, pulling me, feeling me. He's pulling at my bra. My lungs . . . I'm bursting . . . I'm hurting and it's the noise again. The breathing, the breathing, the breathing. It isn't the dream, it's me. If I die now I won't see the children. And what will become of Zee? I need her, she needs me, Zee, help. It's the noise, it's the noise. I won't die.

'Norman. Norm, let her go. Leave her, leave

Shirl alone.'

He stopped then, he let me go. His face was bloody, where I'd scratched it. He was bleeding and swimming away. Tina was in the doorway with the children by her side. As he swam to the metal steps and started to climb up them Tina went for him, she screamed, she punched, she kicked.

I left the old pool by the other steps on the far side. I had blood running down my thighs. My bra was gone, my briefs were torn, I couldn't stop making the noise. I walked round the pool to my cubicle. If I had died Mr Caige would only have his parrot, and Zee might eat even more.

Eleven

'But Tina, why didn't you tell me? Why couldn't you have said? You stole Manuel. You stole my child.'

'Oh shit. Don't keep on.'

'I must know. We have to talk. Why? What have you done?'

'I had to. I wanted it for Al. Pauline had one. Then you got one. I wanted a baby for Al.'

She was in her bed. Her face against the pillow had the same childish look as when she was at the Le Grand and I'd seen her bruises. Baffled, frightened, pretty. Her lip was bruised now as well.

Now wasn't the time to think of myself, about my own pain, my fright, my shock. Tina was ill, I must care for her and comfort the children.

It was Tina who had made the loudest noise, the worst commotion at the pool. She had seen me and the attendant, the man she called Norman, struggling. She had gone white-faced and wild. She knew the man, he was Norm, she had hit at him with her fists. He had retaliated, going for her stomach, she had moaned first, then doubled over and screamed. He'd hit her face then, round the mouth. The cashier heard the noise and come running to the doorway, she had seen the blood on my legs, seen Tina's face, seen the scratched face of the attendant, Norman. She had heard the children's tears. The cashier screamed, raising her hands to the domed roof over us. Some of her pennies rolled into the pool. Norman had pushed past the children. Manuel tried to run at him with clenched fists, Norman pushed him aside. The doors swung close behind his scratched face and ash-coloured hair. Tina turned on me then. I tried to cover my body.

'You been trying to pinch my bloke. I saw. Well he's mine, don't you forget. And Manny's mine as well. You gave up your rights when he got born, he's my child now. Understand?'

I couldn't answer. Of course. He was mine all along, Tina had taken him.

'You been making up to Norm, trying to get him. Just you leave him alone. And leave the kids alone too.'

She had kept my baby for herself, had pretended to me that she'd find another home for it. She hadn't been kind, she'd thought about herself. Manuel was mine, not hers. I had my answer, I needn't seek any more. Here was my child, with me now. My legs felt old and weak. I was with Tina in her home, she was in bed, looking dreadful. The attendant with the ash-coloured hair was her bloke, who beat and ill-treated her. She had tried to avoid me because I might find out, because I might want Manuel back.

'You ought to have told me in France. You must have known that I'd find out somehow. That I'd find the truth in the end.'

'You don't understand, Shirl. I had to. I would of said. I took him to hang on to Al.'

'I trusted you. It's awful to steal a child.'

'You didn't want him. I wasn't stealing, I was helping. You wanted to get out of trouble. I told you I'd help and I did. You were happy at the time, you agreed. You left it up to me.'

'It's not . . . it's illegal.'

'Sod legal. You didn't care. I did it to keep Al.'

'Why didn't you have one yourself?'

'I couldn't. I hate the idea, I saw what it did to my Mum.

'But stealing one.'

'Oh shut your mouth. You didn't want it. I did. Shit, Shirl.'

She whimpered again from the pain of her face, the pain of her stomach, the pain of having to explain. She got out her compact and peered in it. Her upper lip was cut, her eyes looked frantic. She had been no luckier in love than Pauline or myself. She had loved Al who had gone away. Norman ill treated her.

I told her that ice might stop her lip from

swelling. Ice helped you to heal. I looked at her stomach again. The flesh round the navel looked pulped, blood seeped from the edges of the scabs. He had hit her more than once. This was the man she had chosen, who hit her and hit her again. I went to her bathroom; she needed hot water and towels as well as ice. I found a tampon; I was bleeding freely now. I got ice out of her fridge, I put some in a flannel to hold to her lip. I wondered how much of all this Manuel had heard, how much he had understood.

'Thanks, Shirl. You're good. I don't want my lip to show.'

'How much have you told Manuel?'

'Look. You never bothered till you bumped into us on Victoria station. Now you can't leave him alone.'

'I wanted to forget that part of my life, that's why I wanted to write. I wanted to remake my life. Meeting you brought it all back. I can't just blot out the past.'

'Shut up.'

'Does Norman live with you here?'

She put her hand across her eyes. This time she made no sound as she cried. This time I felt no sympathy. She was a fraud, a thief. She hadn't taken Manuel because she wanted him, she had done it to keep Al. She fostered children for the money, their welfare was secondary.

Her home was a shabby one. There was no carpeting, the plastered walls were bare, no cushions, no lampshades, I didn't see any toys. In the kitchen the walls on each side of the cooker had been scribbled over. The children sat there watching me, their eyes distrusted me. I tried to move confidently with a smiling face. We'd all feel better with breakfast in us. We would talk afterwards about what had gone on at the pool, food first.

I could only find two eggs, a corner of margarine. The slices of bread in the packet were growing edges of mould. I trimmed them and cut them, lighting the grill for toast. I'd give each child an egg. Tina and I would have tea. Her bag with the blackened flex of the tea-maker hung on the back of a chair. But for the tea-maker we might all be still at Le Grand. Now all was changed, would never be the same. What did Manuel feel? He was mine, the child of my making, my dark-skinned boy watching me while I buttered toast fingers for the eggs. The texture of his hair was like mine, and perhaps the set of his eyes. ('Dream eyes, forget me not. Love-me-quick eyes.') The past wasn't dead, it was here. What had happened today at the pool would change all our lives for good. I wanted to love him and comfort him. Was Tina lying? Was it true? I couldn't bear to see him tangling and twisting his hands.

'What matters most is you. You must believe that, Manuel.'

He nodded, not speaking, staring, my white-toothed black-haired son. I said there would be no change until he wanted it, life would continue the same. Any alterations, any arrangements, any plans must be mutual

'Mutual?'

'That means helpful. Beneficial to all.'

'Is Norman coming back?'

'I don't know. Don't you like him? Has he always been unkind?'

He looked away, blinking his lashes. Norman made Tina cry. He made her go out at night. They shouted and hit each other. They drank a lot of wine. It was all right till Norman came. Norman didn't like him. It had been Norman who gave him the mask, made him put it on that night. He hadn't wanted to. Norman said cover his black face, take it away.

'One day you'll be proud of it, I promise.'

'He quarrels with Mum because of me. He doesn't mind Lolly, it's me. Because I'm black.'

I wanted to tell him that he needn't stay with the woman who wept and stayed in bed instead of caring about the damage she'd caused. Who teamed up with a criminal, who stole babies and lied about them, who only thought of herself. I mustn't say anything yet. Manuel would make the choice in time. He should be where he could get love. I would be patient. I wanted him with me.

I guessed that it might be Norman when the telephone rang. I stood in the shabby hallway talking quietly.

'Just you leave Tina alone. If I have to get the doctor, it'll come back to you. There are witnesses.'

The same whispering voice. ('Oh Shirley, who's a naughty girl then? I know what you did. I want to be your friend.')

'Look, Shirley, don't be like that. You're imagining things. You've got an imaginey mind.'

'I suppose I imagined what happened at the pool?'

'I never harmed you. You asked for it, you liked it. You scratched my face. Hell cat. What happened was your choosing. You wanted it. I know about you, you know. Swimming in your undies. D'you expect me to beg pardon?'

'I expect you to keep away. For good.'

'Oh no. I know better. I saw you in your skin. You gave me the come on from your cubicle, you peeked. Led me on. I saw.'

'You're a liar. I think you're mad. Tina should take out an injunction.'

'Careful, careful. What's between Tina and I is our business. She'll never leave me – not her. And you and I know what's true and what isn't. I said I had something to say, I wanted to be friendly like.'

'You? A friend?'

'You know about the boy, don't you? That boy you pretended you didn't have, that you gave to Tina. Dirty little hell cat, going with a black. You and Tina, two of a kind, tarred with the same brush. You can take the boy. For good.'

'Go away.'

'Oh I'll go. I'll go. You tell Tina I'll be back

when that boy is gone. Not before. Alrighty?'

He was gone.

'Was that Norm? Let me speak. I must talk. Wait.'

Tina stood in the door of her bedroom wearing her grubby slip. She held one hand to her bruised top lip.

'Go back to bed. He's gone. You're better off in bed.'

'You been saying things. What did you say?'

'I told him to keep away He's a vicious trouble-maker.'

'You don't understand, Shirl. You don't know nothing. He's my bloke.'

She sat on her bed, a leg tucked under her, the other one dangling. Her metal anklet rasped as it scraped the blanket. Her eyes were smudged with tears.

'Why him? What does he do for you? He doesn't support you. You said.'

'I keep telling you, he's my bloke. I need somebody. It's like when I worked for Al. I've had different ones. It's Norman now for me.'

'You mean you give him money? You work for him, you're still in business?'

'Don't you act superior, you've no call to criticize. You were the same once, same game.'

'I'm just asking.'

'You're like your sister, Zee. Just 'cos you changed don't make you no different. You might cook school dinners or book-write. But you done the same as me. Bleeding posh cow.'

'But Manuel? He's terrified of Norm.'

'Manny's all right. Anyway, he has Loll.'

'Not for always. Oh Tina, I don't understand.'

'I feel the same for Norm as I did for Al. I'm not too old, not past it. I kept your kid to hang on to Al. Al liked kids. Norman is different. He don't care for them at all.'

'I don't think you do much. I didn't lead Norman on at the pool, you know I didn't.'

'He can't help his roving eye. Just can't help hisself.'

'What about Manuel? How does Norm really feel about him?'

'He hates him because he's black. Reminds him of me and Al. "He's only half black," I say. Don't make no difference.'

'How do you feel yourself about that? About him being black?'

'I loved Al didn't I? We was special, me and Al. Manny was cute when he was tiny. But Norman can't stand his skin. Can't you understand?'

'I'm trying to.'

'You didn't ought to criticize. You ran off yourself quick enough. You didn't want Manuel, you went. You didn't get in touch. Don't make out you're so bleeding perfect.'

'Where did Al go?'

'Jamaica. He closed the club and went. You can't hostess for ever. I work at nights for Norm. Not always, not every night.'

'You bring them back here? Your tricks?'

'Nothing wrong with that. Norm's here. I was

happy when Manny was tiny. Cute he was. We used to have some laughs.'

'Norman is cruel. Al wasn't. I don't understand, Al was kind.'

'You and your dream talk. "Kind." I get lonely. Norm wants me to himself. Men like to be number one.'

'Manuel is mine. I had him. I can support him. We should discuss it. Does Norman support you at all?'

'He does temp work, I told you. Different pools. He's not a saving man.'

'When did he find out Manuel was mine, that he wasn't yours?'

'When we got back from France. He kept picking on me for going with Al, on Manny for being black. He wants you to take Manny back.'

'And You, Tina? What do you want?'

'Oh shit.'

'Did Manuel only find out today, about me being his mother?'

'Suppose he did. He'll get over it. Norm can't help going after anything in knickers. Norm is a passionate man. That's why he does swimming pools. I knew you liked swimming early or late, I guessed you might be there. I followed Norm to work.'

'Where does Laurel fit in? How does he feel about her?'

'She's temporary. Fostered. I told you. She ain't staying. Besides, she's white. She's Pauline's child. Pauline doesn't criticize, she understands.'

'Pauline? Pauline Jeffcott. From Ladbroke Grove? Why didn't you tell me earlier?'

'Because you're nosey. It doesn't do to tell you anything, you're better not knowing. She's in hospital, like I said. Poor cow, she understands.'

'Which hospital? I'd like to see her.'

'South London. She gets nerves. Depression, nervous attacks. Shirl, I done the best I could. Pauline doesn't know about Norm . . . I only work some nights. I don't want her knowing all this.'

I knew then I wanted Manuel. He'd had too much upset too early in life. The sooner he came the better.

'Hey, Manny, you listening? You eavesdropping, you little pest?'

He came in. He stood by my side, worrying with his hands. His mouth was fixed in an unhappy grin that didn't show his teeth. I said again that what mattered was his happiness, his future, his life. Tina said that whoever wanted him most better have him. When he was tiny he'd been cute.

Twelve

Pauline used to be as striking as Tina in a different way. Her large shy eyes and her way of talking were noticeable. She had come from a moneyed background. 'Lady Posh' Tina used to say, another one too good for this world. But Pauline, in spite of having been badly used by men, kept her expectations and hopes. If you'd stayed patient he'd come. Tina, the realist, said that perfection didn't exist, and who should know that better than the three of us? Our work, night after night, confirmed this sorry fact. Still, you needed someone, a special bloke to love, good luck to Lady Posh. Pauline, after her spoiled start in life, with servants, a governess, had come down in the world with a bump. The man she had lived with had died in a fire, her baby girl died after that. She'd had a breakdown before she came to Ladbroke Grove. I was glad that she had Lolly, another child to love. I longed to see her again.

She used to listen well. I wanted to tell her about Manuel, my newly-discovered son. He was here, living near me, alive, my boy with the dark-coloured skin. I knew where he lived, what he liked doing and how he passed his time. At work I had cooked his dinners, not knowing, little dreaming. I wanted to tell Pauline about Tina, how worried I was, how she'd changed. It would help Laurel to see Pauline. Since the morning at the old pool she'd been even more withdrawn. Perhaps it wasn't so much that Tina had changed but that I had. Norman hadn't been since, nor had he telephoned. She said that as far as she was concerned I could take both of them to visit Pauline. She fancied some peace and quiet. I decided to take Laurel alone.

It was raining heavily when we left. For the first time in my life I had charge of a child on my own. I would cherish Pauline's child, with the quiet ways and honey-coloured eyes. We travelled by bus through the rain. She was in white again with a white bow in her hair, but still rather abject and pale. Manuel had twisted a rubber band under the bow to keep it in place. Her neck was cleaner, her eyes were cleaned free of sleep. She seemed pleased to be in a bus. I wondered if she'd ever forget that morning at the pool and if it would haunt her dreams. She'd just had her fourth birthday.

'Oh Lolly, good things can happen. Life isn't entirely bad. Grow up proud, think well of yourself. You'll see your Mummy today.'

She took no notice but went on chewing her hair. Then she slept, her legs dangling over my knee. I liked feeling her, liked her hot animal smell, mixed with poppy oil. Her narrow feet lay on mine. Her ribbon fell to the floor. The bus windows steamed up as the wheels swished through the rain. I carried her, still sleeping, into the hospital gates.

'She your kiddy?' the porter asked, directing us to Pauline's ward. The Avis was a ward where patients waited until decisions were reached about their treatment, a place of observation and rest. The grounds were criss-crossed with pathways. Signposts pointed the way to the different wards, all with flower names except the Avis. It could have been a holiday resort until you saw the nurses in green and white. A sign pointed the way to Occupational Therapy. Broken lime blossoms lay over the grass, the flowers in the beds were flattened. The rain made a steady sound.

On the steps of the Avis was a red dahlia, its petals squashed and flat. Laurel stirred in my arms and woke up. She'd been easy and light to carry. I put her down and we went in. She had missed smelling the wet flowers and rain-wetted leaves hanging over the grass, missed the sharp greens, the brilliant reds and whites. Her dress was too short and too tight, her boney shoulder blades showed. I'd forgotten the hair ribbon lying on the floor of the bus. The tightly gripping rubber band made a fuzzed tangle of hair round it. She stood rubbing her eyes. No one inside the Avis looked mad. Which were visitors and which were patients? She saw Pauline, her face changed, first disbelief and then a look of joy. She ran to her, Pauline saw her and opened her arms. I didn't like to watch. I felt intrusive. I saw now how like Pauline Laurel was, the same eyes, the same long thin legs and arms, the same fine falling hair. I didn't know what to say.

'It's Shirley. What are you doing here? Why didn't Tina come? Fancy you. How lovely. It's lovely to see you again.'

I explained that Tina had let me bring Laurel because I wanted to see her again. I'd been excited to find out that she was Laurel's mother.

'And you haven't changed, Pauline. Laurel looks like you.'

She said that I hadn't changed either.

The way she looked at Laurel, lovingly, protectively, was beautiful. She mopped at her wet hair, rubbing her thin little hands. Pauline was wearing tight jeans, without shoes. Tendrils of her hair clung to the wool of her sweater. She had never worn jewellery and always the simplest clothes, always looking expensive. She said she'd been worrying about Laurel because she'd had no news. Was everything all right? She'd tried to ring Tina but had got no answer.

'She couldn't come today. She was ill, that's why I'm here. Let's go somewhere and talk.'

A gust of wind blew flurries of lime blossom against the ward window. Pauline took us to the day room opening from the Avis. Dahlias and snapdragons were everywhere, in jars, baskets and stands. It was a pretty room, with matching upholstered chairs where patients could spend time in talking, getting to know each other, mixing. There were playing cards, dominoes, scrabble. You could stitch cotton bags with leather thongs, plait with raffia or make trays with edgings of cane. Idleness wasn't encouraged at the Avis, nor was moping alone. On a table were half-finished jigsaws. There was a buzz of talk. A radio was playing. Only some of the eyes showed why the people were there. In a corner a girl in grey sat with her head in her hands. We sat on a pink sofa under the lime-splattered window. A nurse spoke to the girl in grey, then moved over to us.

'Well, Pauline, is this your little girl? She's certainly worth waiting for. What's your name, darling? Pauline, dear, put on your shoes. You're supposed to be fully dressed.'

Laurel, safe with Pauline, ignored the nurse's question. The two of them were enclosed as if in a transparent cocoon. With faces pressed and hair mingling they were alone. The people, the flowers, the talk, the clatter of teacups and games didn't exist.

I followed the nurse in green. Could I speak please? Was Pauline improving? When was she coming home? The nurse settled her starched cap more comfortably. She picked a pink petal from the table, smelling it before crushing it. Pauline's illness came in cycles. She had been showing improvement. This episode had put her back. She hadn't tried suicide before, that's why they were keeping her longer. She sighed. There was a waiting list. Too many patients, not enough beds, not enough medical care. She'd grown fond of Pauline, rather a loveable girl. Depression was the curse of the age. Single parents were easy victims, they worried disproportionately, became isolated, the children became casualties in turn. Tragic. Staff nurse had tried contacting the foster mother; this person, who called herself Pauline's friend, had showed no interest at all so far. Frequent visiting, contact with relatives and friends was as valuable as any treatment the hospital could provide. Poor little family. It was easy to see what was needed, Pauline missed her child. She sighed. I said that I used to be a close friend, I wanted to be again.

So Pauline was still alone, still awaiting the perfect man.

I went back to the two on the sofa. I told Pauline that I'd been worried about Laurel. She'd been pining, she'd been so quiet. She never mentioned her mother, she hardly spoke at all. Then Pauline touched Laurel's mouth, turning her face to hers, speaking slowly, articulating her lips and tongue.

'Did you – miss – me – darling?'

'Y . . . e . . . s.'

'Pauline, don't tell me Laurel can't hear? She's not deaf is she?'

'Didn't you know?'

'But . . . that's awful. I had no idea.'

'Surely Tina told you? Didn't she say anything?'

'No.'

'She's been deaf since birth. Heard nothing since she was born.'

'Dreadful. It's dreadful.'

To be unable to speak, not to know how was worse than having no one to speak to, the worst loneliness of all.

'She isn't normally so quiet. She's feeling strange here.'

'How will she learn?'

Pauline said that lip-reading took time to learn, sign language longer still. At home with her, Laurel was a lively child. I shouldn't sympathize too much. It wasn't a dire condition, it was sad. What you couldn't change you endured, tried to put to advantage. She'd start at the deaf school soon, her life would improve then.

'You must have been so unhappy, Pauline.'

She said she hated herself for getting ill, for deserting Laurel. When she said this she chewed a bit of hair, like Laurel. Tina ought to have told me, she had obviously neglected her.

Laurel put her hand to Pauline's face, pulling it. 'Ma-ma,' she struggled to say, kissing Pauline's hair. A lime flower fell from her white dress, the stamens making green dots on the pink day room floor. I thought of Manuel. I had a child as well, needing help, needing love, needing me. He wouldn't become a casualty in his turn, I'd make sure. I told Pauline how well he and Laurel got on.

She said she liked Manuel. She'd been glad for Laurel to go there. Some children accepted each other's handicaps without question or notice, they had natural kindness very often. She didn't see much of Tina. They hadn't been close for years.

I told her how we'd met at Victoria. I hesitated. There was something she ought to know. Something to do with Manuel. He wasn't Tina's real child. He was mine. The baby I'd had in Ladbroke Grove was Manuel. Tina took him and kept him. I hadn't known until now.

She stopped rocking Laurel. She stared, her eyes growing bigger still. Behind her another flurry of lime flowers blew against the pane. She spoke slowly. She wasn't entirely surprised. She had wondered about Manuel, had felt something unexplained, a secret to do with his birth. He didn't look like Tina. He had my-shaped eyes. Tina had never spoken about his birth, never spoke about me. He did look like Al.

'He's mine you see. It's changed my life. I'm still adjusting. I'm thrilled. I'm muddled. I'm scared.'

'But he's Al's child isn't he? Al was the father, that's not changed? Manuel is Albert's child?'

'How did you know? It's true. Tina doesn't know. How did you guess?'

'I felt it. I'm often right. I'm sorry about Tina. She's really let me down.'

'She must never know about me and Al. It wasn't serious, didn't last long. Tina has someone else now, a dreadful man called Norm.'

She clutched at me. What was he like? This man, Norman, had I met him? I described his ash-coloured hair, his eyes, his wet teeth and whispering voice. I said he worked in swimming pools, moving from place to place. I didn't tell her about the attack. She went paler still. Laurel's father had worked at a swimming pool, a man called Norman with pale hair, pale eyes and unpleasant teeth. He'd whispered and forced himself on her when she'd been feeling low. She didn't regret having Laurel, Laurel was the loveliest thing in her life. She hated to think about Norman.

Another gust blew at the pane. The needles clicked, cups rattled, jigsaw pieces made small taps as they fitted into place. I was glad Laurel couldn't hear.

Thirteen

'Don't you want to hear about Pauline? Aren't you going to ask?'

'Please yourself. If you want to tell you will. How was she anyway?'

Tina was still in bed when Laurel and I got back, smoking and tweaking her curls. Since that morning at the old pool she had lost heart. She lay in her shabby sheets without make-up, waiting for Norman to ring. Her metal cigarette case with Al's picture was near her on the spread. She hadn't forgotten Al. She must never know about Al and me. Al had been kind in his way. Tina hadn't been the only woman in his life, as well as his wife in Jamaica. I heard he had other clubs, leaving different women in charge. He knew how to please, with chocolates, flagons of scent, kind looks from his kind brown eyes, kind words from his mouth. He'd been proud of his white-skinned staff at Ladbroke Grove, his 'three graces' he used to say, at the same time letting it be known that we were expendable. Tina's men hadn't done much for her, they had used her and left. Norman hadn't even left her a picture. Both Al and Norman probably had babies all over the world.

'Tina, did you know that Pauline tried killing herself?'

'Silly cow.'

'Why didn't you tell me that Laurel couldn't hear, that she was deaf?'

'I didn't think. Tell the truth I often forget myself. I've been upset, haven't I? Had troubles of my own.'

'How could you?'

'She's too young to be talking a lot. She's lazy. Got a lazy tongue. Little pest.'

'If she can't hear she can't learn to talk.'

'Suppose you're right. Shirl, what did you say to Norm? He never rung, you must have said something.'

'Is he all you can think about?'

'He's my bloke. I'm not cold like you.'

Her petulant face was dreadful. I must get Manuel away. I would wait until he wanted me. It was too soon yet. I asked Tina what she thought about me having the two children every day. I'd look after them for the rest of the summer. I liked having them. I worried about them.

'Dare say you do. You and Pauline, two of a kind, both of you Lady Posh, and both wet. There's more to life than cooking and book-writing, more to life than kids. Yeah. Take both of them.'

Her face twisted with dislike.

I had told Pauline about my plan. She said I should be very sure before I uprooted Manuel. Tina might not appear to care now, she could change and make trouble. I should be patient and wait my time. I had found him. I wanted him. I thought he wanted me. She asked me how I felt about him being half-black. I didn't think of him as being any colour, but simply as my child that I wanted to fight for and protect. I hadn't told her about Norman climbing my fire escape or whispering into my telephone, we had already made enough discoveries for one visit. She looked exhausted when we left. She mopped Laurel's tears when we parted, but didn't let herself cry. She stood on the steps of the Avis, waving to us through the rain. I admired and liked her. I had found a friend with a gentle heart.

The children were with me when Cyrus knocked again. Today he was wearing a hearing-aid hooked to the top of his ear, which he kept turned from me, as if he were shy about it. I was glad not to have to shout. I said that I hadn't forgotten him; I'd been busy with the two children. Was he well?

'Gentle, Shirley. I have been lying low. Heart playing up. Blame *anno domini*. I have m-m-missed seeing you.'

'This is Manuel. This is Laurel Jeffcott.'

Manuel, in jeans and teeshirt, was measuring syrup into a pan, having first warmed the syrup tin to obtain an even flow. He was a careful boy.

Laurel was under the table cutting out paper again. Cyrus looked at her. He bent. Engrossed, she hadn't seen him come in. He said something, she didn't look up. He looked very sad.

'This little girl, Laurel, she's deaf, isn't she?'

'How did you guess? How could you tell so quickly?'

'I have experience, remember?'

He turned away again, fingering his glossy hearing-aid. The deaf tended to isolate themselves, he muttered. And the world cut them off. Neglect became mutual. The silent world was the loneliest, the blind or the crippled enlisted more sympathy. In time the other senses learned to work harder, to compensate. You became intuitive with experience. He had known almost at once. I told him that until recently I had thought she was backward, or naturally remote.

'No one is inherently remote. It isn't a natural state. Relating to the world starts at birth. She must learn to get involved. Tell me about her.'

I told him about Pauline and her depressions, how she couldn't leave hospital yet. I longed to tell him everything, about the truth of our lives. So much had come to light recently, I wondered what was in store next. I felt that I didn't need any more surprises for a long time.

To my surprise Cyrus guessed about Manuel. My son, wasn't he?

I told him about my sister Zee. How, after the grammar school, we became ashamed of our home, we didn't seem to fit. Zee married, severing herself. But now she lived near me. I'd had a baby, not knowing that Tina would keep the child herself. I told him about Tina, another undeveloped soul. And yet, she, Pauline and I were alike, in differing ways. Did none of us know how to love? Running from the past was no answer. It sounded a sorry tale.

Cyrus only smiled. He looked older suddenly, fumbling with his hearing-aid. He didn't give any advice. Manuel at the stove dripped patterns from the spoon, the golden trails crisscrossing the syrup in the pan. He sang. He had a tuneful voice. Laurel sat neat as a handkerchief under the table in her clean dress, the paper pieces round her like a lacey edge. Since seeing Pauline she was happier. She looked up at Cyrus with her honey-coloured eyes. He took out his own handkerchief, folding it into a bird shape. He walked round the table flapping the cotton wings. He flapped faster, to the window, round the table, over the syrup pan, dipping, darting, swooping. Laurel laughed, a curious rusty sound.

'I can fly too. Watch,' Manuel said, waving his bare brown arms. Laurel got up, copying him, a sheet of paper in each hand, moving stiffly at first, gathering speed as she chased the old man and the boy. She looked weightless.

'Come fly with Cy,' Cyrus sang in his high, cracked voice. He pointed his slippers elegantly, he reached up his handkerchief bird. His knees and his elbows cracked. Manuel's teeth poked in a smile. Laurel smiled with her eyes. They were being themselves without fear of blows or rows. I had no need to invent a past, my past was my present, here. Then Cyrus took their hands, whirling them round.

'What rhymes with Manuel?'

'Spaniel,' Manuel said.

'Good. What rhymes with Lolly?'

'Polly?'

'Right. I have a friend, Manuel, who's kind as a spaniel. Both he and Miss Lolly shall meet my bird Polly.'

Manuel said that he liked spaniels as well as liking birds. Perhaps Cyrus's bird could teach Lolly to talk. They could learn talking together. Laurel watched their mouths move. She hummed a single note and stamped her narrow feet.

'My bird awaits introduction. He's a personal friend of mine. Let us gather at my place for a cup of Earl Grey tea. In half an hour be in my bower, till then I take my leave.'

As soon as he'd gone, Zee came. I had called her name in the pool, since then I'd forgotten her. She started accusing me before I had a chance to explain.

'Secretive as usual. Why did you run off without saying anything? You might have said goodbye. I worried. For all I knew you could have been battered to death.'

'I was going to contact you. A lot has been going on.'

She looked at Manuel stirring syrup, at Laurel cutting paper on the floor.

'Pardon my curiosity. Just what *is* going on? Is this a nursery school? Do these children live here?

I saw Manuel's face change. He looked anxious, a guarded look. I resolved to keep nothing from him ever. Secrets and deceptions were more painful, did more harm than any truth. I told Zee that the children had become special to me in a particular way.

'Very special, I'm *sure*. I want to talk to you alone.'

'Anything to be said can be spoken in front of the children. No secrets.'

'I fail to see why I should take second place to Tina's bastard child or that fostered brat. I'm your sister, don't *I* come first?'

'Because you are my sister I'll forget you said that, Zee. I'm going to tell you the truth. It will come as a shock. Manuel isn't Tina's child. He's mine. He's my son.'

Zee sat down. Her bottom hit the kitchen chair with a smack. She looked uglier, her face seemed to grow lines. I felt a great pity for her. In a quiet voice I told her about being a hostess with Tina and another girl, Pauline, after I left the school. I'd trusted Tina who said she'd find someone to adopt my child. That person had been her. She'd kept Manuel without telling me.

Zee's mouth set in a line. She braced her shoulders back. She asked me about being a hostess, a life equal to a prostitute. Was that what I'd done in that club? I'd gone with nigger men, hadn't I? Here was the child for proof. Nigger's woman, that's what I was.

She couldn't keep still, she got up, pacing the kitchen. She went into the bedroom, walking from the bed to the desk. She kicked my old sofa, she picked up a blue cushion, hitting it. Go on, tell her the worst. Was there more?

'There isn't any more, not that matters. I have a son. I'm glad. I don't care what colour he is. What does it matter what he looks like? He's my child, he needs my love.'

'Then . . . he's my nephew. What will my friends think? I'm his aunt.'

'Yes.'

'Just like that. No shame. How could you, Shirley?'

'I'm not particularly proud of the work I did at the club. I'm not ashamed either. I shouldn't have let Manuel go. I have him again.'

'You've changed. We've grown so apart.' Her voice had the familiar whine.

I said that I felt she'd deserted me when she married, she'd cut herself off. I'd done the same in a different way by working at the club. I'd had other jobs since. Money and class didn't mean to me what they meant to her.

'My God. What is that boy doing wearing that mask? Ugh.'

'He isn't "that boy", he's Manuel. He's your nephew and my son. Manny, darling, come here, don't put the mask on now. I want to see your face. We both do.'

He struggled as I took the mask from him. I had

never seen him cry. He'd heard everything we had said. His nose dripped, tears dripped from his chin. His cheek felt wet against mine. Tina didn't want him any more. Norman never had wanted him.

Zee watched us. Then, in a shamed voice, she asked Manuel what he'd been cooking.

'Treacle sponge.'

Her face smoothed. She liked sweet things, could she help him? Please? The little girl might like to help too. Ask her now, call her.

'It's no use calling her. She can't hear anything.'

It was Laurel's deafness that started Zee's real change of attitude. Deafness to her seemed the most outcast state in the world, worse than cancer or a black skin.

We went back to the kitchen where Laurel was still cutting paper under the table. By the time the treacle sponge was cooked we were beginning to be united. Zee was beginning to smile.

'What about the parrot?' Manuel said suddenly

'What parrot?' Zee asked

'Cyrus's bird. The bird that will help Lolly. He's going to make Early Grey tea for us. He's expecting us.'

I took Manuel, Zee took Laurel. We went across the hall.

The parrot watched us drink the tea out of Cyrus's black and gold cups. It was an old parrot, with cold round eyes. Nothing was said about Manuel coming to live with me. We knew that he would. It was assumed.

Fourteen

Tina wasn't in bed when we got back. On her shabby pillow was a note written on lined blue paper. 'Gone off With Norm. I won't be back he's taking me to France. Keep Lolly till Pauline gets home. Manny will do better with you. I done all I could. Tina.'

There was no trace of her blue underwear, her plunge-necked blouses or silvery strap shoes. Above the sink on the shelf was a trace of peachtan, some dusty tissues and a chocolate wrapper. Her tea-maker with the blackened flex still hung over the chair. The poppy oil smelled sad in the stuffy air of her room. A broken piece of anklet chain lay beside her bed.

It stayed hot for the rest of that summer. Heat didn't agree with Cyrus, it gave him giddy turns. Games and Earl Grey tea with him and his parrot became a daily event.

Zee got thinner and prettier, we saw a lot of her

too. Pauline started coming home for weekends. I never rewrote the notes, the book never got done. Manuel went on writing recipes and planned to become a chef.

Soon after the dreadful morning they started pulling the old pool down. Sometimes when I look out at the back lane, haunt of rogues, I think I hear Tina's voice but we haven't seen her. Lolly is starting to swim. We go to the new pool now.